Confessions of a Gentleman Killer

Confessions of a Gentleman Killer

A Novel

Johnny Payne

A City of Light Imprint

Published by Blacklight Press
A City of Light Imprint

City of Light Publishing
266 Elmwood Ave, #407
Buffalo, New York 14222

info@CityofLightPublishing.com
www.CityofLightPublishing.com

Book design by H.R. Gordon

ISBN 978-1-942483-94-6

Printed in South Korea
10 9 8 7 6 5 4 3 2 1

For Juana,
my silent partner in all things literary
and the keeper of my confessions

My Confessions

Part I
Kilcairn 1

Part II
Cecilia 37

Part III
Dierdre 89

Part IV
Lois 115

Part V
Mattie 131

Part VI
Valerie 151

Part VII
The Gentleman 195

Part I
KILCAIRN

My best friend serves me a gin cocktail. It's high summer, 1843, foxglove and lamb's ear, London in full flower. Juniper makes my beverage taste mellow, but the cocktail has an edge, strong enough to make me dizzy. I don't normally drink, but I've slept with his wife, so I feel guilty. Dueling is out. He's good with a sword and I am not. The third drink is a newfangled concoction, now laced, I realize too late, with Mrs. Wingate's Soothing Syrup, chock full of morphine. His wife watches him take me down the stairs. She isn't protesting. She knows he knows. Better me than both of us.

I stutter to him there's something I need to tell him and he commands me to shut up. The dirty Thames glitters, as if the streets of Heaven might flow beneath our feet if we stepped on the surface. A policeman asks my escort whether I'm okay. I try to communicate my terror, but the words slur. The policeman laughs and chides us to be careful, the streets are full of danger, and he says I'm lucky to have a friend to protect me from myself, from others. We turn downhill onto an empty street. The best I can do is fall to stop our progress. I only succeed in scraping my leg by tearing a hole in my pants.

He begins to fill my pockets with rocks. He produces a rope and a bag from inside the bin of a seller's stall. A dog trots past, visible in the distant gaslight, ribs showing. The bag is also full of rocks and he ties the rope around both ankles with practiced knots. He drags me into the shallows, not caring that the bottom half of his trousers will get wet. Soon he'll be back at his party, laughing about the new comedian at Vauxhall.

I'm dragged down. I am starting to awaken from the narcosis, finding a rush of strength. But there are too many rocks, and the last draught of air is replaced by brief bubbles in my nostrils, then a rush of water. The harder I breathe, the faster the water invades my throat and lungs. As my brain fades, I remember the women I've killed, trying to recite their names to keep my mind from dying, but they're all a blur, all one woman. The ones I've strangled, it must have felt something like this, only now with water. My feet touch the slimy bottom, and I sink into several feet of garbage, burying me alive, and I realize there is something worse and more grisly than drowning.

Soon I am deaf, dumb and blind, a body, nothing more, spent, dragged slowly along the bottom of the river. A cold and unexpected fish, the kind that can live in this much filth, touches my ear, giving me my last sensation on earth.

Part I

I wonder, as I eat basted eggs and toast, whether this happened. A couple of details are off. I don't have a best friend and wouldn't feel guilty about sleeping with another man's wife. How can I explain my escape from the bag of rocks tied to my ankles? Did the ropes come loose because he was in too much of a hurry? Did I then find a sudden, unbidden surge of strength? Did I really want that much to hold onto life? Did a passing Samaritan mistake me for a good person, one with a clean conscience, knowing nothing of the murders, covering me with a blanket, awakening me with a spot of tea, pepper in the nose, a hair of the dog that bit me?

You, my jury, will pursue me through these pages like a police detective who will judge me and find me wanting. Then again, I will throw you off my track. Maybe I will try to make you love me, forgive me, even hearten me. God knows I need it. Though I try to escape you, we are bound together, so long as we relive these deeds. I can make you my accomplice. I can seduce you as I did twenty women. So long as these pages of confession last, judgement will be suspended, until we know how it ends. Then, you will know the blunt truth—the truth as I say it—and possibly you will bind these pages up—as I bound those women—and take them into posterity. I give a brutal account of myself, one that may satisfy you. Don't pity me. I'd rather you understand me. Don't declare me innocent, unless I am. Saint Augustine says, "The truth is like a lion; you don't have to defend it. Let it loose; it will defend itself."

I'm not a butcher. I slash or I strangle. The branch of my family that worked as Irish sheep farmers quartered plenty of sheep, so I know what the word means. For a century they've drained blood from the throat and cut up beasts for mutton to feed their own, to feed others. Without them we'd all eat turnips and rutabagas and thin out the bloodstock.

That's the real murder, isn't it? To make your people so weak they perish from epidemics. Like the cholera in Soho. A great stink rose up from the Thames. Londoners were in a miasma. When you're used to living in mist, you don't notice it at first. You think your vision is blurred and that the odor is coming from your own body. The women I threw in the river, no matter they decomposed, can't compare to the permanent rotten egg stench rolling off the water, making the air fetid. When Westminster provides a good sewer system, they can complain about me. I'm a fly on the rump of an elephant rumbling through Piccadilly Circus.

I'm better than the last bad fiancé the women had, the one who drank too much and slapped them around; the second cousin a step away from incest; the married boss; the chaplain who blathers about God while he reaches for the wooden buttons of his fly; the good man who speaks of home, work and children because he's dead inside. I have passion and ambition. I could have been in Parliament instead of these digs—I was that close. My mother-in-law Priscilla drew me near. Her tight groin ruled her. Her insatiable ways made her want more than I could give. Did she forget I was married to her daughter Cecilia? That I was in the employ of her husband? That we all had the same circle of friends and associates, lived in the same house? Then again, the last wish of Bellington would be to be buried in a rain of coins. To be mourned by his family, well, that would be secondary.

Now what? Turn myself in? I'm exhausted. I would, if I could find a solicitor of true understanding. We'd talk about French Huguenots, the Edict of Nantes, and the Oath of Supremacy. We'd talk about persecution and what it means to be driven into Ireland because you don't have the right religion, because you insist there's no reason to put a fork on the left side if you're right-handed. I'd give myself up, without hesitation, if a policeman could quote from *The Dangerous Age*, when Elsie writes to Malthe, "Call it madness, or what you will, but I cannot allow any human being to penetrate my inner life."

London Town was mine to give her
Slow sweet river flow
Sun and moon and stars above us
Sweet Thames, flow softly.

That tune I heard from the lips of our constable in the tavern of Carickmannon one night when my Pa sent me to the village square to fill a stoppered pint bottle with beer. I stood immobile amid the smoke and sawdust, listening. I'd heard London spoken of many times in my corner of Ireland, but never with this sort of affection, a caressing voice evoking the surface of a sweet stream. The song had made me want to go live in London when I grew up. It played in my mind during the month I wandered through French burgs where Cecilia was said to have lodged, as I tried to find her, after four years of marriage. None of the tips for which I paid turned out to be true. Or perhaps in my madness I didn't have the wits to locate her.

Provence, with its famed fields of lavender, struck me as an ugly alley choked with ragweed, meant to produce sneezes and watering eyes. Clouds above loomed as pallid swollen faces, ready to spit. The aroma of bread from a bakery evoked a hunger that couldn't be appeased, and I passed by the shop door without even glancing in at the crusty breads that doubtless lay heaped in a basket.

Many a young lady, blonde hair gathered at the neck, resembled Cecilia, as if on purpose, as she crossed the street or lingered to touch the face of her child—the child we never had. After that month, in a fury only the loss of a beauty first held tightly can provoke, I returned to London, to do what, I had no idea. Priscilla and Cecilia had defeated me; it was that simple—the women behind the man.

At the Oxford-Cambridge Club, I had lunch sometimes with Lord Houghton, one of the few men of intelligence there. I thought of one of his poems as I dumped a body into the river flow of the East End, a kilometer from my apartment.

I had a dream of waters: I was borne
Fast down the slimy tide
Of eldest Nile, and endless flats forlorn
Stretched out on either side.

It's a perfect description of the last journey of a young lady, whose name I never learned, only that she was very impressed to be taken to a restaurant with fat shrimp on ice, risotto and a bottle of nice Lambrusco, probably the best that ever passed her lips. She wasn't a whore, just a simple country lass who, when she left her village where the north wind shears the coast, never imagined she'd end up washing other people's underthings for a living. She imagined herself as a prosperous seamstress with a good-looking husband. That's how she described me, as being mighty good-looking, like a Baron—husband material, she shyly joked. I didn't mention the heinous divorce, naturally, the fact that I was a fallen man. It seemed beside the point, to worry her in the last hours of her life. I wanted her to savor the roulade, and enjoy that feeling of getting tipsy, where you begin to let down your guard, as if nothing whatsoever could go wrong, as if you'd just discovered your birthright, like in those melodramas in the theater that Cecilia used to drag me to.

We're told every day in the newspaper that we live in the first age of real human freedom. The gentlemen at the club, half of them believe in slavery still, even though the Abolition Act was passed seven years ago. Only they don't know how to argue for it except to thump the table with emphasis after four or five snifters of brandy, or cups of tea sweetened with sugar made from the mills that turned eighteen hours a day by dint of forced labor. I said to Dr. Chadwick, the noted surgeon, warmonger, and saver of lives, in the midst of his tirade, "No one has a right to kill an enemy except when he cannot make him a slave, and the right to enslave him cannot therefore be derived from the right to kill him." He batted his eyes and replied, "But the slaves weren't our enemies." The conversation moved on to the price of apricots, the use of new techniques of semen analysis to identify the owner of an ejaculation, and the recent run of the decidedly black Ira Aldrige, the African thespian sensation from America, acting as Othello.

The papers call me "the gentleman killer." I wrapped the throat of my first victim in the silk scarf with which I strangled her. That's what passes as a gentleman these days.

I'm also described as "methodical." By that I think they really mean skilled, though they won't say so, for that would be paying me a compliment. I never begin with a plan. A fit of rage overcomes me, when and where I can't always guess. I try to hold it off until nightfall, when the girls are available. Some of them work long hours, and by the time they get off and freshen up, it's not a shop they're looking for. Whores, well they're available round the clock but are for the most part as abstemious as parsons during the day shift. You have to pace yourself, and with people like me roaming around, it's safer to keep your wits about you. Yet by 8:00 or 9:00 of the evening, men going in and out of you all day long, who doesn't have a yen for a pint? You have to numb yourself; kill off those memories; dust off the silt of pain and the feeling that every second of life has been useless. You only exist to please men who can't really be pleased. You swear them off forever and vow to take on factory work, but the next day the same greasy film coats your skin.

Even the prostitutes, I treat each as special. A woman can know she's half used up, that her cheeks are sallow and her breasts not as high as they used to be, but some part of her wants to hear and believe those tender words, and I say them over and over while she protests their untruth. I give her flowers, a bracelet, the things any girl being wooed deserves. If I didn't kill them afterward, you'd say I was the perfect client, boyfriend, husband, or lover. And believe me, that's the man I want to be, the man I tried to be. And failed.

The voice of the angel used to speak more loudly in me before I noticed the lice in its wings. Sometimes I hear it still.

What Kip Bellington and I had in common, besides Priscilla, his wife, and Cecilia, his daughter, was linen. The wet spinning technique had let flax yarn become machine spun and sent thousands of bog dwellers rushing to Ulster. It also put my parents more or less out of business. We sheared hundreds of sheep throughout the year, but despite their appetite for cloth, the Americans didn't want ours; they had begun to make their own. And the blue flax flower, so pretty to the eye, was deadly to us. The rustics of my native Carickmannon and other villages overran the factories, while I hunched over Daisy with shears in my hands until my back ached.

In addition to his imports and exports, Bellington owned a flax yarn factory. The first time I sat down to dinner with his daughter and the family, the table was spread with a cloth of pale Irish green and a subtle design. The Opium War was on with the Chinese—he had a hound in that hunt too, as opium was one of his exports, and the Treaty of Nanking made Bellington yet another fortune. He slivered a breast of roast hen, he raised a cup of Spanish wine, most delicious, and tried out on me one of his memorized Latin phrases, "Bibamus, moriendum est," let us drink, for we must die, and then we clinked glasses. I was only a few days from having Cecilia's shanks wrapped around my waist, her delicious scent of marjoram when she perspired. I took her to a chamber concert, and on the way home, we made a quick detour to my lodging for a fifteen-minute tryst, hot breath on hot breath, and no time to disrobe.

I shan't ever forget the green fields of Carickmannon, emerald, we Irish like to say, that for all my youth spread endlessly around me, like a moldy carpet. I'll never get the smell of wet wool out of my nostrils. Though we were considered well to do, the farm was already going to ruin. I threw my back into my work, stepping around piles of sheep manure in peasant clogs, having to push their hefty bodies out of the way. My only pleasure was Peggy, daughter of one of our ranch hands.

Like me, she was used to wrestling with hundreds of pounds of live mutton, so when things got a little rough between us, she took it all as sport.

As for linen, though, after Kip Bellington exiled me from Mayfair, practically from London, and I found myself ducking into a café off a wet alley to have a plate of pie, a flower girl and I sat at a table with a linen cloth, a brand and style I well recognized. It was one of Bellington's, and for all I knew, the wool had been gathered from my own back yard. I had picked up the young woman an hour before. As the flower girl went on about her mother's chronic cough, and I pretended to listen, I knew that she would soon be gone. If only she had stayed quiet while I remembered Priscilla, my mother-in-law, my left hand wrapped lightly around her throat, how it excited her to feel the slight bulge of her own eyes popping out of her skull. If only this girl I'd picked up had stopped talking, she might be alive now, selling red and yellow tulips at Kensington Station. Maybe all of them would be alive.

Instead, she yammered on. Then she changed the subject, hinting that the hot, glutinous pie had miraculously made her randy. The new tone came a little too late. By then I was already entering a blood rage. We made our way along empty fruit stalls, the sky streaked with purple, only a mist covering us now. The hard rain had gone away. She slid her arm into mine and began to pull me along, telling me how wonderful a scalding bath laced with mineral oil would feel right now. Let's warm our bones, she said. I asked her whether she hadn't somewhere to go, some aunt to visit or girlfriend to cheer up, but she gave a gleeful laugh and replied that she had no one waiting up for her, and that she was as free as the freest bird. I insisted she go home. I complained to her that I thought I was coming down with a cold, possibly the same one her mother had, and she stopped on the cobbles, looked straight at me holding both my hands, and asked "Are you afraid of me?"

I had a woman come in once a week, but since it wasn't Tuesday, that left us all alone. I drew her a bath with eucalyptus oil, and as she disrobed, her smile even a bit shy, I steeped us a tea with hibiscus flowers, which seemed exactly right for her. And there was that laugh again—was it silvered or just tin? With a pert expression, she answered that making tea was woman's work, or servant's work, but she found it a romantic gesture. Her boyfriend scarcely paid her mind. She lay in the tub, her beautiful, pale breasts floating on the water, speckled at the neckline with sun. Her hips were rounded but slender, and the thatch of auburn hair between her legs hovered, expectant.

I told myself that nothing should mar this petite yet robust creature made for birthing sons and daughters, a bloodline that would extend on through the centuries. Were she to live, I could enjoy her many times. Killing her would be like throwing away most of a velvety chocolate cake with butter cream frosting. As she looked on me with soft yet impish eyes, all I had to do was reach down into the bath, as she swooned and nestled against my chest, her bright pink skin prickling against the cloth of my shirt, her moist mouth grazing my ear.

As I watched the flower girl float in the water, as if about to levitate, my left hand found a silk scarf left behind by another date that I had stuffed in my pocket at some point since we entered, possibly while the water for the tea was heating on the stove. Kneeling behind her, I ran my other hand through her copper tresses. She let out a deep sigh, as if she'd never been so untroubled in her relatively short life. With one swift motion of my wrists, the green silk scarf was around her throat, and from there it was just one hard, long pull, as her legs thrashed the water, until she lay still.

The opium-eater feels that over all is the light of the majestic intellect. Those aren't my words; they belong to Thomas De Quincey, our great London writer and addict. I saw him outside the Oxford and Cambridge Club one day, working up the courage to go inside. I had read his *Confessions of an English Opium Eater*. He had no money, and his clothes were a mess. I took him discreetly to a clothier and escorted him to the club for dinner, drawing no small number of stares. Watching him strain not to slump over in his wingback chair, I was reminded of what he also had said: That the natural and even immediate consequence of opium is torpor and stagnation, animal and mental. That's the sickness Kip Bellington and his kind have loosed on the world. They scar the lungs of Chinese and British citizens alike and even missionaries consume the product and help spread 40,000 chests of it every year, alongside the word of God, beyond Canton. His own daughter was one of his victims.

I met Cecilia at a tennis match. To my credit, I didn't know who her father was when I brought her lemonade with frost on the glass. My university mates and I had run down to London for the weekend and it turned into a debauch. We danced the Cracovienne in a hall on Brick Lane full of girls from the silk looms of Spitalfields. As I spun a brunette with a broad Slavic face, I pondered the fact that English weather wasn't good for raising silkworms. Thus, we'd always need the Chinese to do it for us. What had we given in return to that millennial civilization? Half of the young women, liberally doused with the cheap cologne of the month, Winsome Nights or Dandelion Fantasy, were at the dance hall to find a mate, but we'd made a pact beforehand that we weren't there to break hearts. The fellows drank an ill-advised combination of whisky and ale and predictably, two of them ended up later vomiting on the paving stones of The Strand. I was the only one who abstained. They rode me as hard as they could to imbibe, calling me all manner of insults. But I didn't give in. When it came time for prostitutes, and again I didn't want to participate, there was practically a riot about my refusal. They were actually angry, as if I would judge them after. Jerry tried to punch me and the other two had to calm him down—not that his loose swing would have done any damage, even in the unlikely event that he managed to connect with my face.

I'd had plenty of experience with women by then, but curiously, never as a paying customer. So, we went to rooms at the Bingham Hotel. The other three fellows, cheapskates in spite of their family money, wanted all of us to rent a single room and have the women there together, as if it were some kind of strange birthday party. Maybe they wished to watch each other. I really don't know, but I insisted on paying for a separate room. I could never have sex in front of other people.

I could hear the boys in the other room, joking and laughing, the ladies as well, as the males dropped their trousers and stumbled around, trying to get down to the deed, though from what I heard, I surmised that one of them was having trouble, pissed as he was, and the others were egging him on. My girl unbuttoned my cashmere coat, with her face turned slightly toward the wall. I was ready to give her all my attention, as if she were my fiancée, but when I saw her distracted by the cries and pranks of the girls on the other side of the wall, I jerked her head around. "I'm paying you," I instructed, "not them."

I hadn't meant to be brusque, but I couldn't abide to shell out cash for a woman, one I didn't really want to be with in the first place, and have her treat me as an insufferable suitor. That's when I vowed to make her want me. I had her undress herself—she wore a dress of broadcloth, not enticing in the least. She was small in the bust, but had a fine backside. To warm her up, I engaged in some practices that probably weren't the safest, in terms of health, but I wasn't turning back. She started to give the moan that women sometimes make when they're only trying to soothe a man's ego, the better to batten on him later. I curtly said, "Cut out the acting. If I wanted a good show, I'd go back to the music hall." If I'd been drunk like the other fellows, I wouldn't have cared, but sobriety causes a man to be more discerning.

She tried all kind of tricks to make me climax, but I was determined that wasn't going to happen. I held out. If it comes to that, a quick one-off, I could as well have stayed in my clammy room at Oxford and done it myself, without possibly exposing myself to venereal disease. When she was good and tired from her exertions on my behalf, I said, "Lie back and forget about me. You've already earned your money and a big tip besides." The prostitute—Cynthia was the false name she gave, showing no imagination whatsoever—stared out the window with tense longing. I couldn't help but recall De Quincey's phrase from Suspiria, that "in the lovely lady was a sign of horror, that had slept, under deep ages of frost, in her heart, and now rose, as with the rushing of wings, to her face."

My hands moved with tenderness, and I kissed her on the mouth, parting her lips ever so slightly with my tongue. Something in her started to surrender, to go beyond the horror, and I could feel the excitement on her hot skin. I brought her to a brief thrill, the amount of time it takes a cat to stretch, after which she lay still and silent. After a pause, as wind rattled a loose windowpane, she softly said "Thanks," as though I'd offered her a cigarette. We spoke no more. I paid her, along with the promised big tip, she dressed and left, and I also dressed and sat at the side of the unmade bed looking at the dirt rimming my shiny shoes from having walked around puddles, until my mates rapped on the door to call me out with their drunken, hoarse shouts. Cynthia receded from my mind, like a drab wren that darts around a chimney and is gone.

When I met Cecilia, all nineteen years of her, that encounter returned to my mind. I was content at having brought this fetching young woman lemonade. Never had I gazed on skin so transparent, a visage so pellucid and open. "You're sweet," she said, and caressed my cheek.

"I assure you I'm not sweet," I answered.

I wasn't the kind of child who tortured bugs. I was being prepared at school to become a good agricultural servant. In Carickmannon, we were not, as the Tories feared, "fractious and refractory," nor did we read seditious pamphlets or vicious books against Christianity. We were taught The History of the Fairchild Family, which exhorted us to virtue and moral living by showing us pictures of a gibbet and a corpse. Then I escaped. I'd been accepted to Oxford, perhaps on a fluke. The occasional scholarship boy was yeast to leaven the bread of the progressive tendencies they touted. I used the force of my intellect to survive. After I verbally humiliated several of the severe cases in class, and punched in the face a bully who tried to even the score with a physical assault, I was fully initiated. Left alone, I quickly made a circle of mates, scholars and a couple of fun-loving bruisers who took me to taverns hoping that I would repeat my pugilistic feat.

I settled into a low profile. By the second form, I was mostly forgotten, simply one more, as I read with ferocity to achieve surpassing marks. My mother sent me on the side a sum she had saved by exaggerating the household expenses for years and insisting on keeping my father's books.

"Well, no one else bothered to bring me a lemonade," said Cecilia, as I took in the tennis match, trying to understand the rules. "What's your name?"

"Kilcairn."

"Is that Scottish?"

"French Huguenot. I would say it's a bastard dialect, but I don't want to curse in front of a lady."

That witticism got me an invitation to a great luncheon being held the next day, with bloody roast beef, the boldest of red wines from the grapes of Tuscan fields, a spring salad and of course blackberry patisseries. Stout tents had been set up in case it rained, the kind field commanders erect to celebrate with tea after they crush their Indian subjects' latest uprising. Cecilia's father is the kind of man who tries to overpower you at the first moment with his height, manly bearing, and irascible cheer. It seems as though he has to remind everyone within earshot that he's British, no matter that they are too. He's like the man who insists on being called Doctor in the midst of a convention of doctors.

I thought "This is a man who deserves an excellent thrashing, just on principle," but I'd already encountered others like him, and the best thing is to just let them have their way, to a point, until it comes to what matters. Real resistance is quiet, stealthy. Otherwise you're worn out before the real battle begins. The women whose lives I've ended, I sometimes think that if one of them had offered steady, quiet resistance, without making such a show of terror, I might simply have let her go from the sheer originality of it. The impulse to slit their throats came as much from their incipient screaming as from anything else. So I suffered Cecilia's father's condescension as various Wedgwood plates of soulful sky blue and cloud white were brought and taken away, spotted with grease, vinegar, or confected sugar. No doubt he could tell that his daughter had taken a shine to me, so he was firing off a few warning shots about his property, although when he found I was an Oxford boy, his tone changed a bit and he actually sized me up.

"What are you studying then?"

"Law."

"Ah, I wanted to study the law, but I got so busy making money, I forgot to sign up!" This remark was followed by a robust laughter that he could turn on and off the way you might a fire hose.

"I'm sure you would have made a fine attorney, sir."

"Of course, I would. But there's no need to call me Sir. Kip will do nicely."

That's when I knew I had a path to him. There's a kind of man who wants deference, and for you to remember he's above you in experience, but he also wants to be reminded by your manner that he's still youthful.

"Well then—Kip—I hope we'll find an hour sometime to talk about jurisprudence in this great Empire, and the benefits of civilization. Preferably we'll do it over a glass of sherry." I don't really care for sherry, it makes me queasy, but I thought that would be his preferred libation, and in fact it was. I had hit the right combination of deference and bonhomie.

"We shall do just that." Cecilia was forward enough to squeeze my hand under the table, as if we'd already become soul mates. "Thirty-seven Warwick Street, just beyond Mayfair. Look us up when you're next down in London."

On that initial visit to Warwick Street, by invitation of Bellington, I met Priscilla for the first time. She answered the door at once when I rang the bell, as though she'd been standing there all along. The servant woman stood behind her. I was presented with a blonde cascade of hair, bustier-pushed breasts, gown billowy at the bottom but snug at the hips, clear blue eyes made up to look darker than they were. Priscilla dismissed the servant woman, as if she, not I, were the interloper. She took me right through the foyer into a drawing room but didn't invite me to sit down. Instead, she stood directly in front, taking me in.

"Curious," was the first word she spoke to my ears.

"I'm curious? You mean like a curio in someone's collection?"

"I mean I've been curious to know what all the fuss is about."

"I'd no idea I was being fussed over."

"Didn't you? According to Cecilia, you'll be in the House of Commons in five years' time."

"I'm not even out of law school yet."

"But would you like to be?"

"Out of school?"

"In the House of Commons."

I looked away, but when I turned back to Priscilla she remained unblinking. "I hadn't given it the first thought."

"No?" She let an uncomfortable silence set up. Good hostesses are supposed to make it easier on you. Priscilla's specialty was making it hard.

"Many a young man nourishes such dreams," I said, "which then go unfulfilled."

"Why not make them real? Or are you not a man?"

"Isn't that fresh talk for someone you just met?"

"Is it? Cecilia is beautiful. She needs somebody. So do you. And you've got a hungry air about you, so I have a feeling you'll succeed. Here's how it goes. We'll have supper, exchange pleasantries, we'll cagily ask you about your background and upbringing, because underneath, we're already beginning to contemplate you as a possible mate for our daughter. It happens from word one. She had a fiancé back out on her for reasons I won't go into, so she's been hurt, timid, and you're the first possible catch who has made her perk up in several months. You have no idea how transporting one glass of lemonade has made your fortune.

"Kip will take you aside afterward, for—what was it you mentioned, sherry? When he bought a bottle of the best Spanish añejo, I knew he was already thinking of bringing you into the family business. Kip is very particular. He's a good businessman. He'll take you aside after dinner, and treat you in his abrasive manner, but also with brusque affection, to see whether you can stand up to him as a prospective boss and father-in-law. My role will be to entertain you, create a cozy little feeling after the ritual hazing that will culminate in me suggesting that you and Cecilia go out for a walk, enough time to let her set the hook. Make your decision before today is over. Are you in or out? There are several young men, very well connected, with the right surnames, pitching woo at my daughter. They know where the money is. You have the advantage at the moment, but you could easily lose out if you take your time. If either Cecilia or Kip goes cold on you, it will be over. She's just as finicky as he is."

"Do you always talk like this?"

"No. Just this once."

"You make love sound like a base transaction."

"Not at all. Love comes after the transaction, if it comes at all."

"I'm not used to people being so honest."

"I wouldn't go that far. I'm frank."

"Do you love Kip?"

"Of course, I do. What a ridiculous question. There's too much at stake for me not to. Now, shall we have some nice tea and rolls while we wait for Rose to get dinner on?"

"Where is Cecilia?"

"I sent her down to pick out a tart for you."

"I already found one."

Priscilla laughed. I hadn't meant for those words to slip out. But what harm was there in a little coquetry to butter up the potential future mother-in-law, and to soften her businesslike monologue? Somehow, I felt that she'd made me say those words, that she was setting me up—for what exactly, I couldn't yet say. Some women just need hourly attention, and their conquests of men, though constant, are metaphorical. Then there's the other kind—although at that point, I was still emotionally rusticated, Oxford notwithstanding, so I didn't know there was another kind.

Dinner went exactly as she predicted. I slowly ate a succulent Cornish hen, while the others pretended to eat and watched me. I was their meat. They drank lots of wine, pouilly-fumé, with only Cecilia pacing herself. It's a perfect wine for taking the sacrament because it has savor but doesn't stain the teeth; that's why Benedictine monks developed it. I drank a glass for show. If you don't learn to drink with people, you've put yourself at a serious disadvantage.

I told some amusing stories, made up, about my childhood trips to the Cote d'Azur, and how much my father loved sailing. I found myself wanting to slide back into my north Irish dialect but fought it off by peppering my stories with French phrases. I had no idea whether any of them spoke French, but it's always acceptable to introduce that language into dinner conversation in polite society, without being accused of showing off. Anyone well brought up, I discovered, will pretend to understand French. To not do so would be like sitting at the opera in your underwear.

We ate blanched asparagus, wild rice, slivered almonds, and the promised lovely berry tart, with a flaky crust. Priscilla kept her composure at all times, deferring to Kip's burlap phrases and self-involved, half-obscure catalogues of his daily affairs, and a discourse on the effects of the new income tax under Sir Robert Peel.

It was hard to imagine, as I sipped lukewarm tea, that in less than a year, I'd have Priscilla tied to a bed, whipping her hard with a thong, while she cried and alternated between shouting out enticing obscenities, and telling me about the time she took Cecilia to buy a snow globe. I tried not to draw blood, but inevitably I raised welts. I never knew how she explained those to Kip.

After the sherry session and the inevitable cigar—again, I only smoke on demand—Cecilia and I took a walk in the nearby park. She held me by the arm and pressed her body into mine, with a tremble, as we watched a boy in corduroy pants try without success to launch a kite into the air. That autumn evening for some reason smelled like burnt sugar. Cecilia wore a dress of pale lavender. We watched other couples promenade as they laughed and whispered hopeful endearments, real or feigned.

It may sound preposterous, but there is an element of mercy in what I do. I slit the throat with a knife so sharp that death is quick. I sharpen the knife myself, each time. We butchered ours in cold weather. You clean a spot on the neck just above the shoulders. Then you make a deep cut from one shoulder to the other, through the neck. You have to release the animal so that it can move freely as it dies. None of the critics has ever had to force his way through the thick wool of a sheep. The newspapers resort to hyperbole: Police discovered the victim's body by the canal. The mutilated corpse was frozen in a posture of panic, according to Sergeant Billy Club. Intestines bulged from the long gash ripped in the woman's belly. I have never seen a woman's intestines.

After two years and fourteen killings, near the end of 1849, when I was deciding what finally to do about Bellington and whether a permanent solution existed to remedy his and Priscilla's offenses against me, I began to have the distinct feeling of being followed—not by the police, but by someone else. Several times, I wandered into and out of a tobacco shop or café, sometimes with a lady friend, other times alone, only to spy the same pedestrian. Except that it was not the same person each time. Sometimes, it was a man and other times a woman. This is easily explainable, of course, by the simple fact that citizens myself are out in public shopping, eating, or just walking. Yet another's shadow loomed over my shadow. So I began to puzzle over who this person might be, and what they wanted from me.

I remember Peggy, on our farm, squatting on her haunches as we splashed each other with cold water from the trough. She could eat as much mutton or potatoes as me. She had become a woman-child at the age of twelve, and would stay that way, neither giving up one state of being or the other. Peggy did better at sodding a roof than me. When a bird got felled with the stone of a slingshot, you could be sure the shooter had been she. The two of us loved to wrestle, we did it in part to pass the dreary days, filled with mist and cold, splinter and callous, with only the preacher's plaintive pessimism disguised as austere virtue to break off the old week and begin another. Had we not been left alone so much, of necessity, I doubt that we would have passed over into a more carnal grappling. Yet pass over we did.

Peggy knew her physical prowess to be greater than mine. Pound for pound, she was stronger, as well as quicker. Not many boys want to be outrun by a girl, unless she is pretending to flee, as they say, in order to catch him. That sort of ruse didn't interest Peggy. Either you could beat her or you couldn't and no one, in anything, would be given a head start. Perhaps my father didn't watch over us because he thought of her as he did me, his boy. He liked the fact that she didn't come off as "girlish." When she developed "endowments," he ignored them, although he never questioned me when she and I went walking together after dark. Maybe he thought Peggy would break me in, relieving him and my mother from having to do or say much of anything about my passage into manhood. In some sense, she represented a safe bet.

Had I made her pregnant, as seemed likely, that would have been okay. Though my mother wanted more for me, perhaps Pa considered that would be a good way to keep me on the farm, with a new wife he already knew to be one of the hardest workers, male or female, in the county. When things turned out badly, I took a downturn in female company, and got shipped off to Oxford, that departure signaling the end of an unspoken dream.

Two miles from our farm lay a stone quarry, mined out. Over the years, it had filled with rainwater and runoff, tinged pale green from the lime, so that we couldn't see down to the bottom. We really had no idea of its depth. Peggy and I slipped off to it one Saturday summer morning. She persuaded me to strip down, not by revealing her own body, all parts of which I'd seen. Rather, she taunted me until I stood naked. Walking around me, as if performing an inspection, slapping my bottom, giving my genitals a poke, Peggy instructed me to climb up to the highest point of the bluff. When I did, she followed and we stood together staring down into the wide pool. "Jump," she commanded me. I replied that I couldn't for I hadn't learned to swim well. At that moment, she ran toward the ledge and, catching me with one arm, pulled me off the twenty-foot rise. Together we dropped through air, wrapped one around the other. We hit the water hard, breaking the surface and plunged deep, deep, how far I couldn't say. I tried to claw my way to the surface, seeking the air that I never expected to breathe again. Peggy never let go. She could hold her breath a long time, an eternity if necessary. As we slipped apart, and I frog-kicked hard, she grabbed my ankles and pulled me down again, until at last, I pushed her off me with the flats of my feet. I don't know how I kept from drowning, or how I climbed up the moss-slick side to regain my footing. I would have helped her out as well, despite all, but I knew that as soon as I offered Peggy my hand, she'd pull me in again, and the same struggle would ensue.

The walk back to the farm was long. My parents had gone into town on an errand. Wanting to be left alone, I stalked to the barn to begin some neglected chores. Peggy followed me in, laughing and boisterous. When she tried to kiss me, I grabbed her by the hair, threw her against the grainy planks of the barn wall and raised my hand to give the first blow.

In a single month, I graduated and married Cecilia at St. Magnus the Martyr on Lower Thames Street. A gilt archangel looked down on us from either side with a saturnine expression, while the pipe organ throbbed like God's last headache. Bellington cried behind his hand, and I thought that maybe he'd changed his mind, wishing he'd bet on a different horse. Priscilla embraced me for far too long, pressing into me like a practice bride. The next afternoon, there was high tea at the house, with finger sandwiches and scones. This was a new custom, brought into vogue by the wife of the Duke of Bedford. Now we all must do it or perish. She said that in the long breach between luncheon and dinner, she got a sinking feeling. I know just how she felt. The high tea was a relatively small affair, just enough guests to provide Kip with an audience. He used the occasion to spring on me, in public, his proposal.

"Kilcairn, what do you know about exports?"

"I know that they must leave the country." Laughter came all round, except from Kip.

He persisted. "What I mean is, we're short a man or two at Bellington and Makepeace—and by man I mean manager."

Cecilia leaned against me. She still had the scent of a newlywed clinging to her, and her face was besotted with joy. The offer just made by Kip represented the jewel in the crown of her happiness. Everything was now officially under wraps. Priscilla looked on with vampirish alacrity, silently reminding me of our conversation—according to her, our pact. Yet I had begun to have other thoughts on the matter. "Well, sir—that is, Kip—it sounds inviting. But I had been thinking about maybe joining a firm or starting my own little practice."

"What?" He looked as though he were about to strike me a blow with his fist. Taking in the company around, he settled himself. "This is the first I've heard about it."

"I've only begun to contemplate my profession. I graduated less than a month ago. That's why it wasn't mentioned before."

"Certainly, I have plenty of connections in the legal world, were it ever to become necessary. We have a need for counsel but first you must learn the business. Shipping is more complex than it seems."

"I'm sure that's true." Once again, Priscilla did nothing to take me out of my discomfort. Nor did Cecilia, for that matter. The Bellington family gave the impression to the invited guests that I had sprung on them a nasty surprise. "It was just an idea."

"Ah, at twenty-four we all have big ideas. And, of course, you just took your degree, so you're full of the law. I think you'll find what I'm proposing far more rewarding."

"No doubt I will. So, when do we start?"

That evening, Priscilla found a way to get me alone by "showing me around"—guiding down the hallways with me, the new son-in-law, who'd been in the house many times. In the bedroom that was now to belong to Cecilia and me—she backed me to the wall and said, "I'm glad you didn't make a scene. Most attorneys are parasites, and poor parasites at that. You were made for something nobler." Having said that, she slid halfway to the floor, holding to the sides of my silk shirt like the rails of a greased ladder, her blonde locks spreading over my trousers. I can't recall whether I enjoyed it. I was busy smelling the vapors of mothballs that had been keeping in storage Cecilia's trousseau, the one gotten together for that other fiancé, the one who ran away.

Less than a week later, I lay in bed, Cecilia in my arms, watching a green moonrise, striated by the open blinds. The clop of hooves announced a carriage beneath, and receded. The elm outside housed a dove that purred now and then. Everything seemed to smell of leather in the house, even our room, as if it were a tack shop. That's why I left the window open. I thought otherwise I might suffocate. The décor had been made for a man; it was hard to imagine Priscilla in charge of those furnishings, high quality but blocky. There were two beds in our room, neither quite large enough for two people. I could only wonder whether Bellington had some strange need for appearances. At first, I thought it a custom, or that he and his wife, long married, had separate mattresses. But I saw through their bedroom door that this was not the case.

The clock's tick at length sent me off to sleep. I awoke half an hour later to Cecilia shrieking and shaking in my arms. I tried to comfort her. She clawed her way out of my arms and sat up. Footsteps came thudding down the hall and our door flew open. There stood Mr. and Mrs. Bellington, all got up in plush pajamas. Bellington's eyes bulged, and he looked at the empty bed, then mine, as if utterly surprised to see bride and groom on the same side of the room.

Instinctively, Priscilla put her hand on his chest and whispered a phrase in his ear, at which point Kip left the room. Sweeping past me, she sat beside Cecilia, stroking her long, lank hair. Cecilia's sobbing had become a series of broken sighs. Soon Bellington returned with a spoon and a bottle of serum. Cecilia sipped it and calmed down. At first I'd thought it was a tonic for cough, but soon enough I realized it had to be laudanum. So Kip's opium trade reached all the way back to his own door.

As if reading my thoughts, Priscilla said, "She suffers these attacks now and again. They have nothing to do with you. She only needs the medicine on occasion." I wasn't prepared to make any comment on the laudanum. I couldn't puzzle the thing out, yet I had a suspicion that the old fiancé was involved. This was a matter I resolved to speak about with Priscilla when the first natural opportunity arose. The rest of the night I held Cecilia, stroking her face and waiting for the dove to coo again.

I began working at Bellington-Makepeace, at the wharf. Sailboats and steamboats came in and out of the harbor ceaselessly. It was a traffic jam at all times. Even the steamboats had sails, because they used huge amounts of coal and it was expensive. I watched the coal heavers, still half-black with soot, stagger onto the dock looking for a fast pint, the first of many they'd drink before the day was over. I heard one of the sea captains quip, "If they didn't drink so much, they'd be of very little use." Seamen were as important to the East End as the aristocracy to Westminster. Traffic had risen fifty percent over a normal year, so the business had become unusually profitable, and Bellington looked almost giddy as he paced the docks.

I was first put to use as an accountant, a task for which I had no training. The math, though tedious, was fairly simple. I could have done my job from the house, really. Then Bellington began to move me around, supervising this and that group of men; even having me go into the ship holds to inspect cargo and make a report of any spoiled or subpar crops and animals. This in particular put me in Bellington's good graces. He asked me whether I had direct experience with such things, and I answered all I had was good instinct. City inspectors existed for these tasks, but they were constantly being bribed. The wharf became one long scene of intrigue, whether it was dust-ups among the casualty men, a ship that suddenly caught fire, light horsemen thieving from ships at night, or women selling fruit and vegetables from barrows. It was the first time I heard a woman shout, "He's my man," in a context that wasn't romantic.

It became clear that Bellington was giving me a run-up for taking over the business someday. I found it touching to see this more vulnerable side of him, however tacit. I found it fatiguing just to watch him get through the day. Part of him wanted to treat me like a son, and part of him seemed to detest me.

Cecilia fell into the round of accompanying her mother to charity concerts and luncheons. Like me, she was being taught to "oversee"—in her case, the house servants, who must have found it irritating suddenly to take orders and suggestions from a girl whom they had bathed and perhaps even nursed. Cecilia tried in all ways to act as a cultivated person. I caught her reading some of my books, especially Descartes' impenetrable Dioptrique, as if the secret of life resided there. She perused that tome over and over. I only half understood its pages.

She also devoted herself to the piano. I can't say that she was exceptionally talented yet, as in all things, she persevered. The girl had a special touch with Chopin's Mazurka in A Minor. What a relief that was from the tedium at simply being alive in the world. Shrieks at night had lessened considerably. I dared to believe that she felt contented.

If sin is weakness, rather than bad intentions, then I am a sinner. I don't consider myself religious by nature, but we must have something to call our horrid behavior, and the word ethics doesn't get at the deeper truth. All that term means is I knew something was wrong and chose not to do otherwise. Maybe that's why everyone goes to church. Every time I looked at the altar, I felt like I was back at my own wedding ceremony, only this time as a spectator.

Cecilia's mother sent her to Northampton to help tend to a sick cousin for a few days. Priscilla made it sound as though by going, she would be performing a patriotic duty to the nation. Cecilia threw a fit. I did take her side, patiently stating the case to my mother-in-law, who appeared to agree with me. When I returned from work the next day, however, my wife was gone. I suspected that the bottle of laudanum accompanied her on the journey, in a leather pouch on the floorboard of her train car.

The next day, I came down with the walking flu. I assured Bellington that it was not a problem, and that of course I would accompany him to the wharf offices. But Priscilla had other plans. She insisted to her husband that it would be cruel to force me to that zoo of ships—besides which, it would only prolong my sickness and make me lose more days of work as a result. She knew which lapel to grab him by. This was the age of productivity, possibly the greatest era in human achievement, and each of us played a critical role in the unfolding historical drama. The only things that could stop us from being greater than the Romans were business taxes, inadequate trade treaties, and odious officials. That's what Bellington had read in the latest treatise of the Private Law Chamber.

So stay home I did, with no wife to tend me but instead a mother-in-law. Carrying a tray of muffins, cantaloupe, and juice, she entered my bedroom with the stealth of a grave robber entering a crypt. The window was opened a crack for fresh air, but the curtains remained closed, clinging against the screen like a stocking to a woman's leg. She plumped the pillows, straightened the rumpled sheets, smoothing them down with her pale hands, and laid one palm on my forehead. She said, "Your face is hot"—no news to me, as I had spent the night sweating.

Priscilla offered to give me a sponge bath. I declined.

I pretended to be asleep when she returned with a washbasin, sponge and towel, as well as fresh robe, but this ruse didn't slow her down. She unbuttoned my pajama top and soaped the hair on my chest. I was weak, to be sure, but found within me a surge of strength. All at once, I lunged at Priscilla, wrapping my hand around her throat and squeezed it hard. She gave a surprised cry of pleasure. The longer I held her in my grip, the more she gurgled with desire. Her hand slipped under my waistband.

I loosed my chokehold. "You've already betrayed yourself," she said.

"Let go of me. There's something I want to ask you."

"What?"

"You put Cecilia on the train."

"Did you think otherwise? Anyway, that's a statement, not a question."

"Who came before me?"

"Mohammed, Isaac Newton, Shakespeare."

"What I mean is, was Cecilia a virgin when I met her?"

"Aren't we all?"

"I'm not joking. Let me be more direct. Did she get pregnant by her fiancé?"

It was the first time I saw Priscilla slump. "Does it matter?"

"Or put another way, did she get an abortion?"

"You're so tedious."

"Answer me."

She sighed. "Yes—by him. And yes—but before the quickening."

"I hope you took her to someone knowledgeable."

"Why, so she won't be damaged goods? Neurasthenia is his specialty, and he knows our daughter well."

"So that makes it legal?"

"They revoked the death penalty for that procedure a decade ago."

"Well then, no one was at risk. That's a comfort."

"You're no judge to moralize. After all, the Greeks and Romans did abortions. That should suit a high-minded individual such as yourself."

"I should have been told. If nothing else, as information."

"We had to. She had become a mental wreck."

"And she's not now?"

Priscilla threw the sponge into the basin. "You can wash yourself." With that, she left my chamber. I spent the rest of the day tossing, until I got up in early evening, in fact, to bathe myself. The scented water felt good against my skin, ridding me of the pasty sensation.

The bedclothes had been changed while I bathed in cool water. I put on fresh pajamas and fell asleep. The wind began to blow the other way, so the curtains billowed over me, as if Saint Michael had arrived for an annunciation. Instead, in came Priscilla again. The walls glowed twilit, first mandarin, fading to the color of the cantaloupe I'd forgotten to eat in the morning. She lost no time in shedding her clothes. Her body was gymnastic yet round at the hips and bosom, with a waist that could only be achieved by bloodstock or fanatical exercise. I thought she cinched, but it was all her. She straddled me and placed one of my hands where the hip met the waist. Within seconds we were glued together, her pitching and rocking.

I panted like a street dog thrown a rasher of raw bacon. "Where is Kip?"

"At the club." Now her hips gyrated, as she worked to

close the deal.

What most sticks with me about that encounter is the ferocity on her face, as it caught the last shafts of sunset before the first gray of night covered her eyes. I would have thought she hated me more than anyone she'd ever met, though I couldn't think what I had done to deserve it, except betray her daughter.

So began our tryst in earnest. We took to meeting at an apartment in Hampstead, on average twice a week, though sometimes more. I'm not sure who it belonged to, maybe one of her friends. It was beautifully appointed, the kind with clocks and carpets, faux-Chinese furniture that cost more than the original, and maple blinds on the window. I clapped my hand over her mouth, to keep any stray neighbor from coming around, and then that became a thing in itself. Predictably, a riding crop was introduced, ropes and gags, clamps and masks. From there, it devolved into a steady, gentle degradation befitting aristocracy.

This is the way a certain kind of woman binds you to her. Never having been given the freedom and consent to strike, I found it exhilarating at first. This was far different from giving Peggy a smack. It came with cashmere before and cologne after. There was always balm to salve the wound, heirloom porcelain, a plush patterned Turkish carpet on which to lie back. Yet after a time, the masquerade became excruciating, as I came to see that there were many rules. Behind the animal grunts lay an invisible conversation about propriety. When she got me to read a book by De Sade, I found the writing laughable. I couldn't get beyond the first few pages of his pretentious philosophy, his proverbs worthy of a Liverpool fishwife: "Sex without pain is like food without taste." What is more, I didn't want this to become a self-conscious exercise in art.

I threw away the tools and the books, and we were left with the naked struggle, the art consisting of our own oaths and curses that could be mistaken for affection. She was trying to wear me down, but I showed just as stubborn as her. Our fight code was even more minimal than that of bare-knuckle Jack Broughton. I would return spent to Cecilia and her tremors, knowing that she wanted more and that I was leaving her unsatisfied. But I could find no middle ground. I had to be at one extreme or the other, and Cecilia couldn't stand up to the rigors that came naturally to her mother. Besides, we lived in her parents' house.

One of the reasons I could meet Priscilla in Hampstead was because her husband rented me an office there. He took me out for a meal of sausage, eggs and whisky—a man's breakfast, he called it—at a tavern; the roughest place we'd ever eaten together. He had another proposal.

"How would you like to become your own boss?"

"I don't follow."

"The railroad. There's excellent money to be made there over the next few years."

"What's the proposition?"

"Some associates and I will set you up as the head of a company selling shares for railroad lines we plan to lay down in less traveled parts of England."

"I know less about selling than I do about accounting."

"You're a quick study. The company will be put in your

name, but my partners and I stand right behind you."

"To whom will I sell shares?"

"Mainly the customers will be merchants, teachers, and tradesmen. As for the stock brokering, we'll get you licensed as quickly as possible. I can pull strings there. You'll become the head of a railroad at twenty-five years of age!"

"One that doesn't exist yet."

"Of course, it exists! Papers have been drawn up, and soon, we'll stand in awe of trestles, rails, and beautiful stations with marble counters and a clock at the top."

"And this is legal?"

"Right now they're drafting new laws about the railroads. Everybody wants to get in on the action, even the MPs."

"I'll turn it over in my mind."

"Sure! Think about it. We'll have a smoke tonight and continue the conversation. For now, digest those bangers. I've gotten an eye on an office space in Hampstead. You'll love it there."

I did my checking. I hadn't practiced law, but I hadn't trained for nothing. Parliament had already passed more than one hundred Acts about the railways that year alone, and it was only June. I would pay myself a salary. We had a stock exchange; that was no issue. It had existed since our first Elizabeth had put it there. Besides, Kip was like the robber who accosts you on the corner. You see him holding his bludgeon in hand, you know you ought to cross the street, yet you walk past him anyway, and get whacked.

PART II
CECILIA

BEFORE I KNEW IT, I HAD BECOME AN ENTREPRENEUR. As I walked streets, sat in the homes of families, met groups in the church or schoolhouse, these bland, trusting, industrious faces looked as familiar to me as those in Carickmannon and its surrounding countryside. They slaved and saved, praying to the distant bishop of the Church of England for good crop yields, withstanding blights and the cripples in their flocks. Good citizens, patriots, devout and credible. When I left Ireland, I had never wanted to see their like again, yet they roamed the East End of London, these sons of Japheth, only their accents and clothing changed.

I asked Bellington to take me to one of the sites of these planned railway lines, where we supposedly had right of way. He took a day off and we repaired to the site. I gazed on the desolate bog.

"London once looked like this," he declared with confidence.

I had a knack for sales. People found me "honest," "down to earth." It reminded me that I had once sat humbly in a schoolhouse, doing my sums, with a vague idea that I would uplift humanity when I grew up. Cecilia, who up until then had mostly served as a ghost presence in my life, all of the sudden turned assertive.

"Father says you're making lots of money, for him and for yourself, and that he's very proud of you."

"Anything for the family."

"Yet don't you grow tired of the family? Living among them? "

I enjoyed the tact with which she brought up the subject and decided to make it easier on her by finishing her thought. "Darling, it's time for us to move into our own place."

She was choosing a shirt for me to wear, stroking the front as if it were a cat. "Really?"

"It's what married people of means do."

Cecilia flew to me and hugged me with unsuspected strength. "It's what I've wanted. But I didn't know that it meant so much to you as well."

"I want us to have a life apart."

"Then you'll tell them in the morning?"

"We'll tell them in the morning, together."

That night Cecilia brought to the living room two cups of chamomile. She had understood that I was not a great lover of alcohol, and when with me, never suggested it. Sitting on the floor together, we stared into the empty hearth as if it were wintertime and logs blazing. For a moment, I could imagine myself as a child again, how my mother slept in a room separate from my father and would keep me abed with her under the pink chenille bedspread. A calendar graced by a corn maiden, many years out of date, hung tacked onto the wall, and I wondered why no one ever changed it. I would listen to my father snore through the other side of the wall, his Scotch-settled brawn making it impossible to wake until morning. My mother would put me to sleep with the story of Fenris the wolf who could break the strongest chain yet be bound with a silken thread.

Cecilia leaned against a hassock eyes closed. "I was engaged once."

"It's not unusual. You married me."

"But there is more to it than that." She began to weep ever so softly, as if she were humming a tune she'd forgot. "Poor Kilcairn. We've trapped you like a bee in a bottle."

"Don't say that, my love. I'm here because I want to be."

"I wished you'd met me a year sooner. I was the biggest catch of the season. Can you believe it—his Christian name is Wilberforce. His father serves in Parliament, so he's unimpeachable. The first time we held hands, he had on kid gloves and I ones of calfskin, so our fingers didn't actually touch. He actually bowed. I guess they had taught him those manners in the Naval Academy. He's the sort of young man who people call 'smart'—a reference to his dress, not his brain. When we rode horses together, at the end of our ride, he dismounted me, and I sat in a stand meant for a small crowd, but it was only I. I watched Wilberforce perform dressage. You know, the jumps, making the horse prance in a certain way, quarter and drill—all that.

"He was set for a big career as an officer. His father wanted him to go into politics, but he was willful. At first, I found him terribly real. Unlike me, he pushed back at his parents. For that alone I would have followed him anyplace. Often, we spoke of Africa, and though he seldom smiled, it made him laugh that the only question I asked was whether I'd get sunburn there. But it turned out he wasn't so real after all. For all his formality, he took my virginity on a cot in one of the stables. He sent the stable hand off with a quid to get drunk with some mates, leaving us alone. I won't say he was violent—he tried to be nice, after the military manner, asking before he groped. Wilberforce was just—indifferent, clumsy. I hadn't lain with anyone, yet I somehow knew he wasn't very good at what we were doing. Afterward, I said, perhaps with slight sarcasm, the kind my mother uses all the time and me practically never—I said. 'I'll bet you're talented at badminton.'

"He must have taken my meaning well enough, for he stalked off, leaving me with my dress unbuttoned. But he came back, because that's what you do in his world, up to a point. Loyalty and all that. We kept on with the engagement—the same soirées, the same friends. Every once in a while, we'd repeat what happened at the stables, only now in a room rented by one of his pals. Nothing we did was sordid, but he managed to make it seem that way. Then I got pregnant."

"Cecilia, you don't owe me any explanation for anything. It isn't as though I'm a virgin either."

"Yes, dear husband. But this is what happened to me, and I must tell it. I got pregnant. Though no one had enlightened me about the facts of life, I knew something was wrong when my monthly time didn't come. People think because your family has money that you know certain basic things, but I certainly did not. I dared not tell my mother or father. I confessed to Wilberforce, whose first reaction was disbelief, after which he asked me whether I'd had romantic encounters with any of his friends. I pretended not to be insulted. He sent around one of those same friends to take me to a physician. In short, the doctor confirmed that I was indeed with child.

"That night, as we supped broth, he delivered a long speech about responsibility, quoting Vice Admiral Horatio Nelson. I remember clearly what he said. 'The lives of all are in the hands of Him who knows best whether to preserve it or no, and to His will do I resign myself. My character and good name are in my own keeping. Life with disgrace is dreadful.' Wilberforce never had an original thought, but at least, I said to myself, he is handy with a borrowed phrase.

"The next day, he posted to India, for a spell of duty. Then I was forced to tell my mother. I hoped to be able to keep the baby."

"I wish you had. I would happily have taken his place as its father."

"Would you?"

"You and I could have a life like anyone else's. Having a child should be the most normal thing in the world."

"And you wouldn't be afraid?"

"Of course, I would. But I'd have to get over that, wouldn't I?"

She took my hand in hers. "That is sweet of you to say. Only if I'd had the baby, they simply would have given it away. As it was, they sent me to Italy. My mother said the Italians were more understanding about those things. I resigned myself to carrying my child to term. But one day my mother showed up, wearing black. She's just that unsubtle. Back to London I was whisked, into the hands of what she called 'a highly competent physician.' After that episode, my father was desperate to get me off his hands. Then you came along."

Violence welled up in me, the nastiest kind, as I imagined Priscilla in false widow's weeds, giving orders. I forced myself to remain calm, for Cecilia's sake. "Is that it, dear wife?" I uttered at last. "Are all your secrets told?"

"Are you angry?"

"Not at you."

"The pain was so great, they put me on—well, opium isn't the elegant word, but that's what it is. In this house, you get a free lifetime supply. Just because a physician costs the most doesn't mean he's the best."

"We're going to get you help. I know a doctor certified by the General Board of Health. He doesn't prescribe preparations that contain mercury or arsenic. Or recommend a change of air, vomiting, bleeding, the power of prayer."

"I trust you. Whatever you recommend, I'll do it. Did you really mean it—about us having a baby?"

"Yes."

"I don't know—after what happened—even if I still can, physically—I don't know if I can stand up to the rigor of it."

"It's not something we have to decide about right now. Let's go to bed, my love."

"Did you know that they don't tie you down in those mind hospitals anymore? It seems the new thing is to let you roam around, so you'll feel free."

I took her off to sleep and as she dozed, I pulled up the sash and for the first time in my life, smoked tobacco because I really wanted to. Any strong scent would do to kill the leather smell of the house. The green moon didn't show in evidence, just the usual leaden London sky, so present that one forgets to look at it. I tried to make out one cloud from the other, but even in the glow of distant gas lamps on the bridge, it appeared a solid black mass. Cecilia jerked awake with a shriek. I jumped from the sill, ran to set the chain on the inside of the door and braced my body against it, planting my bare feet on the wood floor so they wouldn't slide. I heard footsteps running down the hall, and felt a blow as the door rattled in its jamb.

"What in hell's pantry?" It was the first time I'd heard Bellington curse. "What's going on in there?"

"What do you think?" I answered. "The usual."

"Well let us in."

"Leave us alone. I can take care of my wife."

A befuddled silence followed. "Very well," she said. "We'll see you at breakfast."

In the morning, as promised, Priscilla awaited Cecilia and me. She sat on the piano bench, as if Cecilia might take a sudden urge to jump on it and play one of Mendellsohn's *Songs Without Words.* It was only seven o'clock and she perched fully dressed and made up. The hired girl tried to bring breakfast into the music room until Priscilla scowled her off. Uncertain, the girl left the tray on the settee and scampered. Bellington was nowhere in sight.

She didn't waste any time. "Where, pray, do you suppose to live?"

I waited for Cecilia to speak up, take her part, but she only looked at me with a slightly sickened expression, as if she'd eaten a sour plum on an empty stomach. "We might rent some rooms for now."

"Why don't you get on a work gang while you're at it? John Stuart Mill would be thrilled. His philosophy should suit you, because he's big on hedonism and he believes that animals have the same moral standing as humans."

"I don't disagree with him."

"Go out, the two of you."

"I assure you I plan to rent something decent, a town house. Your daughter will be taking no longer a step down than when she married me."

"That will surely qualify as the most disingenuous statement of the day."

"And if we like it, then of course we'll buy."

"Yes, mother. I'm sure we can find something close by." Cecilia was winding herself up to apply logic to the situation, to meet her mother in the middle, to be reasonable and pull away by increments so that it wouldn't be felt as abandonment. The only way that Cecilia had the slightest chance at success was to tell Priscilla right out to go fuck herself and punctuate the phrase with a solid backhand. I couldn't help but smile recalling the secret vellum emblazoned with bawdy phrases that got us boys through many a dull Latin class at Oxford.

Non sunt in celi
quia fuccant uuiuys of heli

The monks are not in heaven
because they fuck the wives of Ely.

Before Cecilia could reach for her mother's hand, Priscilla used that same hand to push her daughter backward, so that she stumbled and almost fell, only catching her arm on the sideboard. It was at that moment Priscilla lost the battle. Cecilia didn't look all that surprised, only hurt. Blood throbbed in my fingertips. I knew that if I so much as grazed an inch of Priscilla's skin, I wouldn't be able to stop until I had broken several bones.

"We'll be going. I'll need to separate a temporary lodging before nightfall." No way I was going to leave Cecilia alone in her mother's clutches. She might easily send her off on a train, as she had before, or lock her in the pantry like a bag of rice.

"You'll go nowhere," said Priscilla. Neither of us bothered to refute her.

"Cecilia won't be taking laudanum any longer. I am legally in charge of your daughter. I am her husband."

"You work for my husband. I'd say he's in charge of you."

"And I'm making him a lot of money just now, so that's not a long conversation."

"Good luck with Cecilia. I think you'll find that certain tastes get in the palate, and you can't get rid of them, no matter what you do."

"Bad habits can always be broken with the right effort."

"Can they?"

We rented a house in Chelsea, on Sloane Street, from a man who was taken with a fit to move to Germany, although he held onto his property in case things didn't work out. Germans now represented the epitome of health. That first night, my wife made egg salad with turmeric and it turned out she was partial to dark ale, but didn't dare drink it at home, so that's what we dined on while we sat on the balcony huddled together under a blanket to wait for a falling star in the smoky sky. Strangely, I enjoyed the ale like no beverage I had ever sipped.

She went to an auction and bought the contents of the house of a woman who had just died. Cecilia moved the furniture of someone else's existence into ours, not assigning a spurious emotional meaning to inanimate objects. I didn't mind sleeping in someone's bed, as long as I didn't know whom the previous owners were, but some details did strike me as distasteful, such as a brass spittoon that sat beside an easy chair.

Thus, we had our nest. Cecilia did not in fact have to be interned. I hired a physician who came to the house thrice a day, as well as a stout nurse with nimble hands, and Cecilia began to withdraw from the opium. I had grown used to her sudden shrieks before, so those didn't unnerve me. I found it useful in my career as a killer to be able to tolerate the shrill screams of a woman begging for mercy.

Once Cecilia was cleansed of her habit, she moved back into our marriage bed—that is, the bed of someone else's marriage, now ours. She showed a touching gratitude in her every gesture. She cooked for me flaky pies stuffed with tender lamb's meat and leeks, one of my few happy memories from Ireland. She bought new dresses in the mauves and soft greens she had noticed I was partial to and I took every opportunity to compliment her appearance, even asking her to wear her hair down in the house, pulled back with a simple bow. In the bedroom, I let myself enjoy her giving that favor no man will reject. I could detect hints of the same ravenous appetite as her mother's, waiting to be unleashed. She suspected I had been more assertive with other women. She didn't know what exactly lay inside the box of treasure, but she wanted the lid sprung and would pry it with a letter opener if necessary.

I wished to transport her there and knew it would be good for the both of us, as we lay eating a sorbet in the midst of a heat wave. Yet there was something about Cecilia—not virginal, it would be laughable for me to use that word regarding my own wife—but maiden-like, her long, lank blonde hair only emphasizing this. The best thing for both of us would have been to indulge every appetite, ensuring that I wouldn't fall back into a trite and questionable tryst with her mother. Yet Cecilia, despite her great efforts, couldn't shake giving the impression of a woman caught in eternal convalescence. In the same way you can't quite convince yourself of a fat man suddenly grown slender, I couldn't accept entirely that she had passed over into permanent health.

All the same, by some measure the months that followed could be called divine days. Cecilia set herself the task to learn French. In the midst of cloudless days of sunshine, she would announce "*Il pluit ici aujourd'hui,* drawing a laugh from my lips. Or from the bedchamber she might announce, "*Je suis deshabillée,*" coming out to beckon.

In the evenings, we began to read *Candide* to one another. She surprised me by her gusto for Voltaire's satire, revealing a mischievous side of herself under the right circumstances. One of her favorite passages was when Candide slays two monkeys following two damsels, only to discover that they were the women's lovers. Hearing her unexpected peals of joy, I asked what in particular so inspired her laughter.

"Don't you know, dear Kilcairn? In this part of the story, you no doubt imagine yourself to be Candide. But in fact, you are one of the monkeys."

For an instant I was taken aback, for yes, she was right; of course, I would assign myself the leading role. Seeing the mirth in her eyes, I said, "Dear lady, I accept your judgment."

"You needn't worry. Only look at what his companion, the wise Cacambo, has to say. 'Why should you think it so strange that there should be a country where monkeys insinuate themselves into the good graces of the ladies? They are the fourth part of a man as I am the fourth part of a Spaniard.'"

"Also being the fourth part a gentleman, I won't dispute your finding. However, may I point out that the ladies are not only monkey lovers, they are cannibals."

"Likewise, I accept your judgment on me."

I kept hoping she would become pregnant. The idea took hold of me more strongly than I would have guessed. I imagined it would give Cecilia and me a center to our lives, making the others around us seem less consequential. In the evenings, even if I arrived tired, we walked for half an hour around the neighborhood, as she pointed out things she noticed, such as a certain black and white stray cat with one eye who slinked along the ground until it gracefully hopped on the back of a bench and walked it with delicate paws, moving its head slowly from side to side.

"She has one eye but sees more than anyone in the park."

Time passed, and a baby didn't come. She never brought up the matter and I didn't dare, except to comment on a happy-looking couple with a buggy, looking down into it as into Christ's manger. I continued to wonder whether the abortion had caused some permanent damage, and finally I returned to that question. "There are good surgeons who might have an idea about what to do."

"Yes, I've thought about it. But I can't abide the thought of any doctor getting near me in that way, not again. If nature wants to give us a blessing, it will. Did you notice this lady is now weeding her garden with great abandon? Either she's fallen out of love with her husband and uses it as an excuse to get out of the house, or she's fallen madly in love again, and wants to cook his favorite supper."

Part II

Railroad stocks had tripled in value in a year's time. Bellington and his mates crowed, elated. I seemed the only one made nervous by the prospect. Something about it didn't square. I'd had to hire two assistants, as it was no longer possible for me to go around knocking on doors, so the sales fell to them, as I managed our growing assets. One day, in came a fireman, ashy face and bedraggled eyebrows, telling me that he had seen a little girl burned alive as she ran out of a house. He'd rushed to wrap her in a blanket, but it was too late and she died from the burns that day. That same girl had come to him as a phantasm, to prophesy to him that an earthquake would open up along the rails, twisting the iron and swallowing all. I was about to explain to him that it was physically impossible for the fault lines of earthquakes to run exactly parallel to all the railroad tracks in England for hundreds of miles, but realized that this clarification was a waste of time, so I simply refunded his money.

I decided to visit Bellington at his home to speak about the overvalued stock. All of us owned plenty, on paper our fortunes were made, yet none of the construction had begun on any of the supposed railroad lines—so in fact, even if there had been an earthquake, nothing could be destroyed. I'd begun to get a few calls about it from these small investors, and so far had made up excuses about permits, drainage, and any other nonsense that went through my head. The company had been created in my name alone, so there was no one else for them to talk to. Improbably, the company was worth over 80,000 pounds without a single trestle having been laid.

When I arrived at 37 Warwick Street, after sending a note to Cecilia that I'd be detained at her father's house, the hired girl answered. I could hear Bellington's boom of a voice within, making what was no doubt light conversation—his friendly volume lay just short of a yell. She came back to ask if I could return in an hour's time. "Can't I just wait inside until he's ready? He is my father in law and I did live here once," I explained, absurdly, to a servant who knew me well and for whom this was not new information.

"I'm sorry but missus emphasized that you were not to come in just yet. I really do apologize."

I was on the verge of pushing my way in but thought better of it. Perhaps they were having a marital discussion and didn't want me privy. So I walked around until I became bored and popped into an apothecary's shop for a headache remedy diluted in seltzer. When I returned, the door to 37 Warrick sat ajar.

I entered.

I shouldn't have felt surprised that Priscilla sat alone in the drawing room, reading a ladies' novel, *Coelebs in Search of a Wife*. "You sent everyone away."

"They had things to do."

"Leaving only us."

"I suppose so."

"Say what you have to say, Priscilla and I'll return tomorrow."

"Let me serve you a whisky."

"You know I don't like to drink."

"Yet you force yourself. I admire that. Shall I give you a neck rub?"

"I'm perfectly fine. I drank a diluted powder from the apothecary's and it's starting to take effect."

"You could have chopped your head off with a guillotine, so

it wouldn't bother you. You're just like a character in Pixérécourt. *I awaited death daily, hourly, in the blood stained capital. It can easily be imagined that my thoughts were of the deepest black."*

"I don't go in for dramatics. You know how much I hate it when Cecilia drags me to those dreadful melodramas."

"I'm only saying, Kilcairn, that I can imagine you beating a dog to death."

"You say that because I've beaten you. But I'd never be that cruel to a defenseless animal."

"Speaking of defenseless animals, how is my daughter? She doesn't visit much, unless it's with you as a chaperone. I hear that you've maintained her sober."

"I flatter myself that she's happy. You should be proud that your son-in-law looks after his wife. I bring her a bouquet from time to time; I make sure she's well cared for. She doesn't want for money or affection either."

"Tomorrow is Cecilia's birthday."

"I plan to take her out to Mélange in Chelsea."

"It's all about France for you, isn't it? Perhaps you and Cecilia one day will find occasion to travel there. I hope you don't mind that I sent her gift over a day early, in fact it was while you idled at the apothecary."

"Why should I object to you giving your own daughter a present?"

"It's just she's been so long without laudanum."

I slapped Priscilla, releasing the ball of my fist into an open hand at the last second; otherwise it would have been a punch. As it was, I could hear knuckles crack against the bone beneath her eye. I should have left at once, to keep Cecilia from opening the packet of opium, if she hadn't already. But already Priscilla's fingers grasped at my bone buttons, she knew I'd gone stiff, and she pulled me for the first time into the bedroom she shared with Bellington. I'd never so much as set foot there. For all I knew, he or the house girl could return at any moment; it wasn't beyond Priscilla to invent a pretext for them to be gone for an hour and take pleasure from their sudden return and our mutual ruin.

As I battered her body with mine and listened to the headboard knock against the wall, my mind, always active, contemplated that the headboard would scotch the paint and Bellington would notice it, if not at once, some evening as he removed his robe. How could he not? Yet that was the least of my worries. I had recklessly bitten my lover's face and throat and her right eye had already swelled half closed. Why is it that smearing our sweat on each other, feeling our skin tighten as it cools, licking the salt off one another, brings such pleasure? Why did she insist on burying her face in my damp armpit as into a branch of honeysuckle? I began to heave as if I were going to vomit, but nothing at all came up. I felt quite sure that as we lay with Bellington's blue sheets wrapped around us like sentient climbing vines dragging us to the floor, Cecilia lay strewn on a couch, eyes rolled back, tongue wet, drool on her neck on the day before her twenty first birthday.

For a moment, I considered snatching up a paperweight from the night table and smashing Priscilla's skull with it. I could easily imagine the mixture of bone fragments and blood pooling on the pillow beneath her. I would reach inside the shattered cranium and caress the brain as it throbbed its way to extinction. It was the first time I ever truly wanted to murder someone.

Using that trite phrase that we employ to segue from the basic agony of sex, she said, "What are you thinking?"

"About us," I answered.

"How like we are?"

"Yes—like a wolf and a house cat. They're both carnivores. Yet you only dare to put a bell around the neck of one."

"You or me?"

"I don't know yet."

"Kilcairn, I want you to stand for a seat in the House of Commons."

"I'm not a politician."

"Nor were you an accountant or a salesman. As Kip always says, you're a fast learner. Those were never meant to be permanent posts. I talked to Kip about it, and he agrees. With your blazing intellect, you'll catch everyone by surprise. You've made your associates a lot of money, and surprisingly, you have a good touch with people when you discard your arrogance and put your mind to work on work. It's a long shot, but we think you can pull it off. Kip has many powerful allies, and the Prime Minister is trying to flood the House for certain reforms he wants to undertake."

"Why doesn't Kip stand himself?"

"He doesn't like the limelight, unless it's in a small group of people. He is aware that he seems ungainly in public and prefers to remain connected indirectly. There are trade tariffs pending that could change his shipping business significantly. A lot of money is at stake, and he needs every advantage."

"I see. Why didn't he ask me?"

"He thought you'd say no."

"And that you are more persuasive."

"Aren't I? Think how happy you'll make Cecilia. It's what she's always wanted for you."

I expected to return to the Cecilia of glassy eyes. A cheerful wife met me, blue pupils shining, as she embraced me and said how much she was looking forward to a tender cut of prime rib and a bottle of cold champagne tomorrow. If she smelled the wrong scent on me, she didn't mention it. She could have been too busy doting, or it could be that her mother's skin on mine had the same chemical consistency, thus the same fragrance as Cecilia's and mine.

"I brought you a silver charm bracelet." I had stopped at a jeweler on the way back and spent an excessive amount on this trinket, in addition to the gifts I was saving for the next day. I presented her with a wrist decoration in which each charm was, or would be, an icon of my guilt, for I knew that I would now lie with Priscilla many times more, risking everything to experience a draught of nausea that I somehow mistook for happiness.

"Did your mother send over her present?"

"I threw it away."

"I have an early present of my own for you. I'm standing for the House of Commons."

She flung her arms around my neck. "Darling, what wonderful news you've brought! I dreamed of it since first we met."

"I still have to win the seat."

"Is Daddy backing you?"

"So it seems."

"Then you're bound to win. Generally, he gets his way. He just wears people down."

"Well, it appears that we are all to act as one happy family again. I know estrangement from your mother has worn on you. But take care. I find that when we draw too close, bad things start to happen."

Part II

The morning of Cecilia's birthday, I decided to waylay Bellington at the wharf. In the midst of the noise of the harbor, ships blasting their horns, seemed a much more promising place to converse with my father-in-law than the deadly still of Warwick Street, where screams could punctuate the illusion of peace at any given moment. Kip looked none too happy to see me. Since Cecilia and I moved out of the house, he'd had little to say and when he visited my offices, it was to look at the balance sheet and keep me up on the latest bills being debated in the House of Lords.

He slammed the door. I'd never noticed that he'd hung an oil portrait of a Negress behind his desk. Or was it new? Had it been pegged there as an abolitionist statement, or the opposite? Was it a cry for human freedom and possibility, or just the gauche fantasy of a middle aged man? Her upper body was massive, as if carved crudely from a vein of coal by a child miner, and I couldn't help wondering whether Kip dreamed of being crushed inside those limbs. "Sit down," he said.

Clearly, he was annoyed beyond his usual irritability. I considered asking him what was wrong, but with Kip, it's better not to announce your intentions in any way. You let him make the first move, the second, maybe even the third before truly responding. It's different with Priscilla, where you spar and either party is capable of throwing a knockout punch at any time. It's like Ben Caunt defeating Bill Brassey at Six Mile Bottom. Everyone talks about the fact that the fight lasted 101 rounds. But it could have lasted one round and either opponent could have taken the other down at any time. Each man reached a fever pitch over and over, becoming subdued in between, to survive, but always dangerous, always ready for the next blow.

"I may have to bring you back over here temporarily. You did take the bar exam, right? We've gotten involved in a lawsuit with some disputatious Norwegian shippers over lanes and rights. The Prime Minister of Norway is threatening to step in."

"Maritime law may lie above my level. I barely know how to argue on land."

"Nothing lies above your level, Kilcairn. That's been my experience. You'll stretch as high as you have to."

"I serve at your pleasure."

"I don't trust the attorneys I have. They bungled a case and it cost me ten thousand pounds. I need someone in whom I have utter faith. And that is you, son."

"Do you draw a lot of lawsuits?"

"You have no idea. It's the price of doing business."

"Have your other attorneys draw up a brief, if you don't mind, and I'll read it right away."

"There's the man. Naturally, you'd have to keep the railroad concern going. You'd have to do both and that would mean more hours."

"I'll do what's best for you. But is there going to be a railroad after all? I've some clients who are beginning to get annoyed."

"What a question. Of course, there will be. We just have to clear up some preliminaries. Landowners need to be paid off, et cetera. Anyway, why should they complain? They're all making money. The stock market is in paroxysms of plenty."

"Yet it can't last forever."

"That's what they said to Jesus Christ."

"You do know that I've agreed to stand for the House of Commons."

"Yes, glad to have you on board. I guarantee that you'll win. You've had more success selling shares than anyone else

I know in the game. You've turned out a genius and that has made you some well-placed allies."

"I wouldn't call myself a genius."

"There's that becoming modesty. That will stand you in good stead during the elections. You can't miss."

"Cecilia's birthday is today."

"Is it? How is she doing?"

"You should come over and see."

"That wasn't my question."

"We'd like to have you and Priscilla join us for dinner at a very fine French bistro."

"I've been living on sausage and beef jerky, bad tobacco, and vodka. I don't think my stomach could take anything less damaging."

"If you change your mind, we'll be at *Mélange* at eight."

"You owe Paris no reverence."

"There's no principle involved except my palate."

"Something troubles me, Kilcairn and I need your advice. It's not about the business."

"Anything you need."

"Shortly after I left yesterday, Priscilla got assaulted."

"In her home?"

"Yes. I find it hard to believe, but she let a man in who claimed he had something serious to tell her about our daughter. She's not usually credulous, but he tried to rape her, from the looks of it. She has bite marks on her breasts and neck and her left eye is swollen up to where she can barely see out of it. I'm sorry to go into this vulgar detail, but there it is. You're a member of the family so I thought you should know. You can understand why we won't be joining you tonight in a public place. I don't even want Cecilia to see her mother."

I looked into my ale as into a murky crystal ball. Bellington, for all his awkward bluster, might stumble into the truth if I let him. I wanted to berate him about neglecting his daughter, but I knew I had to watch my step. "Did she call the police?"

"I was going to, but she begged me not to. She didn't even want me to fetch the doctor, instead putting a cold compress on her eye. I met his steely eyes, but said nothing.

"Come on, son. Surely you have an opinion. Don't you care about your own wife's mother? Priscilla must mean something to you."

"Give her what she wants."

"Do you think so?"

"It's my opinion."

"I'll take your advice. If I had caught him in the act, I believe he would lie unconscious in the hospital right now, or in the morgue."

"Doubtless."

"The funny thing is, I don't think this is the first time he's crossed her path. I've found scratches and bruises on her before."

"How odd."

"You'd almost think she enjoyed it. Either that, or she is the clumsiest person in the world."

"I wouldn't call her clumsy. She said that you and she used to dance in the most posh ballrooms in the city."

"Used to. At the beginning, before she bore Cecilia. So you agree with me that there must be some other reason why my wife keeps coming up with contusions?"

"I'm only listening to what you say."

"You needn't worry, Kilcairn. I have lots of time to lie in wait for this abuser. He'll turn up again. And when he does, his suffering will begin. In *The Factory Strike,* that play Priscilla took me to at Royal Victoria, they murder a perfectly good factory owner, a man generous and kind to his employees, and they burn down the factory that gave them sustenance. They might as well have killed their own father. But in the end, there is retribution. There is always retribution."

When Kip asked me to take on the Norwegian case, I devoted several nights to understanding charter party law and its international and local implications. The matter had to do with a seemingly minor technical point to charter parties, which nonetheless affected large sums of money. I argued successfully that in certain cases, even if the signatories were not of our country, English law could legitimately be included as binding background law, and London could easily serve as a relatively neutral site for disputes. Bellington worked through part ownership in some companies and brokerage firms based abroad not bearing his name, and found yet another way to increase his earnings. I'd made him happy and he had no more to say about bruises or retribution.

Cecilia had made a house party for Thanksgiving, complete with a stuffed bird and latticed pies. The fall wind had stuck just enough ice on the windows to make a becoming sheath, through which the glowing logs of the fire could be spotted by each of the small circle of friends we invited to our gathering. Cecilia insisted on taking each of their coats and laying them neatly on our bed, instructing me to pour mulled wine into the mugs she had purchased especially for that occasion. The very smell of the roasting turkey brought everyone under the spell of the hostess's charm, sealed by a smile that, I was reminded, beamed more beautiful than that of any other woman. Part of that beauty was its sheer transparency.

Life had inflicted on Cecilia wound after wound, me not being the least of them. Yet she had somehow gathered it all into a silken coat, which she wore lightly, with the conviction, as she might put it, that our existence is ultimately something good and that humans are noble creatures, despite whatever actions they may take. She served potatoes and cranberries, hot rolls that burned her thumb, with complete ease and confidence. I'd never seen her so strong, so full of grace and homey elegance, setting down the plates in an ongoing swirl. To my eyes, she figured as a drawing that can only be made in one continuous line, the artist never lifting up the chalk until the portrait is complete.

As we continued to drink wine, mixing talk of politics with jokes and gossip, Cecilia also told several amusing stories about her childhood, which she bathed, for the purposes of that meal, in a golden glow. Her father was a loveable curmudgeon, her mother a wily but good-hearted task-mistress. Not only did I not contradict her; it gave me pleasure to listen to her reinvent her life, assigning it the meaning she wanted it to have. Everything seemed to lie in her capable hands that day. Cecilia even allowed herself a smug expression as she lifted the empty plates after the last pots and chafing dishes were scraped clean, and still people wanted more. She had satisfied.

"Now," she announced, "Contrary to the prevailing custom, we are not going to break off into two groups of roosters and hens, so that the one may speak ill of the other.

This is Thanksgiving. I invite the gentlemen to light their pipes right here, while we ladies fan the smoke away with our dirty napkins. And while that is going on, with the help of a bottle of good brandy for you all, I am going to express my thanks on this day with a song I have composed for my husband, which I will now play on the piano."

Lifting the cover, as I received prematurely admiring glances, Cecilia sang with a lyrical resolve and a fluency of tact on the keys, the like of which I'd never witnessed before.

Just as I touch the soil beneath a rose
To know whether it needs a drop of water
So do I spread my arms and hold him close
To see whether a kiss will bring him laughter.

Sometimes a shadow falls upon his brow
When woes of work and life have brought him sorrow
We wander where sweet hyacinths still grow
And let the twilight sweep us toward tomorrow.

The thrush warbles its lilac morning song
Made from the syllables of one man's name
Like me, it trills the word Kilcairn, Kilcairn
The small blue soul inside a yellow flame.

I was stunned by the subtle poetry. The surprise, beyond her sentimental composition, was in its performance and piercing effect on everyone, most of all me. As Cecilia ran over to lean against me, asking "Did you like it?" and our friends radiated approval, I was overcome with an unaccustomed shame. I knew I wasn't the man in the song, except that's how Cecilia saw me. I didn't deserve this woman, yet she was mine. I was trying to be a better man but would always fall far short of that rhapsodic vision she released into the room, on that most perfect of nights.

"Yes. Out of the poor clay of a man you wrought a priceless porcelain urn."

"Don't be silly. All I did was look at you and wrote down the first thoughts that came into my mind."

Does anyone believe in the reality of his own death? I know I don't. I only imagine myself stalking someone or other through eternity, trying to remedy an inscrutable situation to which I can't give a name. The first time was when my cat was torn to pieces by a marauding fox on the farm. I studied its minute corpse and wondered whether in fact resurrection was possible, as was preached by the village vicar every Easter. When I asked my father about it, he replied with an expletive and went back to repairing a broken hinge on the gate.

He was fierce, my pa, brawny and taciturn, a farmer everyone was slightly afraid of, even though I never saw any actual violence from those rugged arms. He would sit for long periods in the evenings, before a fire, reading treatises on husbandry, as his approach was scientific. I would creep up behind his chair to sit on the rug, for some reason imagining that this mostly peaceable father would grab an andiron and begin to destroy my mother's porcelain dishes and the portrait of her grandmother that looked like a mad gypsy about to cast a spell. By the time my mum was rubbing the soles of my feet and stroking my legs with her blue-veined hands, telling me how handsome I was and how I would break many a girl's heart with my devastating beauty, Pa had wandered off to bed in a room down the hall, austere, its walls entirely bare, and with a straw tick on the floor like the ones used by peasants.

I was prone to catarrh, so Mum rubbed my bare chest with a paste of herbs in the evening, commenting on how muscled I was for my age and telling me that someday a thatch of hair would grow on my chest and belly. The truth is, I was sickly, and only the rigors of tending sheep and helping rebuild fences kept me strong while I waited for adolescence to supply the invisible muscles that my mother foresaw. In fact, it was my mother who gave me to our teacher. Tillie was her name, a single lady who stayed clear of the local bachelors.

Mum bathed my limbs and the rest of me, anointed my ash-blond ringlets with oil, put on me a new pair of thick-soled shoes, so the wool socks wouldn't get wet in the puddled ruts, and a suit of linen, as if we were about to go to a Sunday bible lesson. She swore me to secrecy beforehand, telling me that Pa must never know of this impending visit, because his attitudes were medieval. I had no idea what "medieval" meant, but it didn't sound good.

When we arrived at the cottage of Tillie, sprinkled about with bluebells, she received us and gave me a cupcake and a drop of whisky diluted in lemonade. The woman smelled of some exotic plant that would never grow in the cold rain of Ireland and her bosoms were pushed together by a girdle that made them more conspicuous than when she taught us in school about the invasions of the Protestants and the meaning of geometry. While Mum sat primly on a willow branch sofa, Tillie took me to a back bedroom, with a bedstead covered with a white spread, removed my shoes and clothes, and kissed my skin in many places until I grew agitated, as if I'd been stung by bees. She drew me close, opening her legs, inviting me into what I can only describe as a maw, and pushed on my back until I began to shudder. I squirted something into her and her fingers relaxed, sliding off my shoulder blades.

Afterward, the three of us sat at a table in her dooryard eating a beef stew with corn cakes, while the two of them laughed and chatted about the various ailments of their neighbors and discussed how to cook kale so that it wouldn't taste bitter. My mother asked me whether I'd had a good time. When I blurted out "Yes," they laughed again, in a different way, their voices more high pitched and tears springing to their eyes until they sighed and were still and quiet. Mum thanked Tillie for her hospitality, and I did the same. We visited Tillie a couple of times a month, until I fell in with an older girl who had dropped out of the school and worked in her father's tavern scrubbing down the slab counters and carrying ale to the rough men whose shirts were permanently bedecked with straw.

In my run for Parliament, I met with Makepeace, Reynolds, Stansfield: Bellington's most direct business partners, as well as with several current members of Parliament. We had a lengthy discussion about an impending Piers and Harbours Act, as well as Mussel Fisheries, Sugar and Buckwheat Duties, Prisons and of course Railway Sales and Leases. Wherever there was a shilling to be made, that's where they turned their attention. These men ran the British Isles. I wasn't the only person they had recruited. This group possessed financial interests everywhere.

They operated in the legislative realm on a slim majority that was eroding and were mustering all their resources to essentially take over the House of Commons.

To some extent, I understood what I was getting into, though I can't say I could see too far into the torrent of rain. By becoming an MP, I felt that over time Cecilia could get out from under Kip and Priscilla, that I could begin to make my own alliances, and would in that way become independent. It never seriously occurred to me to just start a small law practice, as I'd always wanted, live modestly and forget the rest. I began following the legislative process in detail, for the first time ever, and was interested in relief for the poor, reform of the lunatic asylums, and of course, legislating a massive improvement in the sewers and sanitation of pestilent East London.

Before long, I was being trumpeted by Bellington's people as one of the great financial wizards of the decade. Surprisingly, no one contradicted this preposterous claim. There were too many other candidates associated with dubious business and political dealings for much of a harsh light to shine on me. With this advisory group, mostly I stayed quiet, and in public gave modest speeches peppered with occasional tart remarks that caused knowing laughter, and I seemed ready to inherit a role in London government and society.

At the club, I became noticed in a new way. Members treated me with strategic warmth, figuring that I might have favors to bestow in the future. Cecilia wanted us to make the rounds everywhere. In spite of her natural reticence, she enjoyed watching while members of the public approached me, smiling, taking my hands, sending drinks to our table, asking my opinions about issues of the day. I kept expecting a blow to come, but despite the fact that Bellington paid me almost no attention, he and his associates were sheltering me under an invisible dome. I had become used to his abrupt manners, his casual negligence about personal matters, his insular ways, and the fact that on some level, neither Priscilla nor Cecilia nor I existed for him. He was scarcely ever to be found at his own home those days, and had rented a small apartment closer to work, where he often spent the night.

My sexual craving for Priscilla had never ceased—I admit it. I tried to placate that bestial desire by pressing on Cecilia certain acts I needed. At first, she was receptive. She could see where we were headed and didn't seem to mind although mostly she was trying to please me. One day, returning for lunch, I caught her gazing in the mirror at finger bruises on her shoulder, running her nails along her skin as she inspected the small marks I had made on her. Her eyes brimmed with tears.

"I don't think I can do this anymore," she said.

"I apologize. They're just little bruises from where I was holding you tightly."

"These in themselves are nothing, dear husband. They don't hurt. Only I know where all this is going to end. I can feel it rising up in you. And I'm scared."

"Say nothing more about it. I promise to treat you gently. We have more pressing matters to think about, such as how you're going to manage as the wife of a politician."

She brushed my chest with her fingertips. "I wish I were somebody who could stand such things."

So when I told Cecilia that I was getting an apartment because of constant work obligations, she didn't object. "I think it's a wonderful idea. That's just what Daddy is doing."

All the logistics and finances of our railroad business were run by persons beyond my station. And mostly I filled that time with carnal congress—specifically, sex with Priscilla. She had me over one morning for a late breakfast. "You're a public man now. You can't afford to be caught out with other women, and much less with prostitutes. It could ruin your career before it even gets started."

"I do have a wife, you know."

"I hear you're becoming a bit of a brute."

"I didn't know the two of you had gotten so familiar again."

"We're trying. It's never too late to improve our relationship."

"I'm glad for you."

"Your rough energy can't be expended on that particular person."

"What do you suggest?"

"The most practical solution lies in your mother-in-law. The two of us being seen together is the most normal thing in the world."

"Yes, I can see your point."

"After all, who but the most depraved subject of the Queen would suspect or accuse such a pair of any relation beyond the most innocent?"

"No one except a lunatic. So it's okay for me to consort with a whore, just not a prostitute?"

"Exactly. It's the best thing for you, me, Kip and Cecilia. Everyone wins." She had already begun to undress, treating me to a slow revelation. What we did next can be described in a single word: everything. Only I took care to leave no marks. The two of us came to be experts, with a forensic precision, in concealing the corporal evidence of our deviant practic-es. Besides, according to Priscilla, Kip never touched or came near her at that time. The embers of their marriage had gone cold. Since the incident when her eye was blacked, she said, he had lost his appetite, although she still desired him. That may have been part of why he took an apartment elsewhere—to avoid her demands, and in case something did happen to her to replace his absent affection, he didn't have to know. Suddenly Priscilla and I had almost unlimited freedom. Many nights we spent together, as the election approached.

I was obsessed with seeing her. As soon as we parted, I had already begun calculating the next meeting. Even the little time I had to spend working and campaigning felt oppressive and unreasonable, and I had to make a great effort not to utter curt remarks when I was interviewed by the newspaper or asked to participate in a debate about the new educational system and whether it would promote a greater civic spirit among the vice-ridden and criminal masses.

Then it happened. The election loomed, less than a month away. In a single week, stocks in the Great Eastern Railroad Company fell ten percent and the plummet continued the following week. A panic began and predictably, large amounts of our railroad stock, which I had long known to be overvalued, began to sell off.

Bellington and his mates were the first ones to unload their shares, just before the panic began. I couldn't get in touch with him. No one, not even Priscilla, could contact him for several days. Then we got word he was in Manchester and would return on the weekend.

Like an idiot, I maintained my loyalty to our non-existent railroad. I tried to weather the drop. As the panic increased, I too sold my shares, which by then had lost more than half of their value. I'd been preparing to buy the house we'd been renting for a year. Bellington had told me nothing in advance.

Angry investors stormed the offices, demanding restitution, as the stock's value decreased almost to nothing, and my company had to be declared bankrupt. Before long, a number of lawsuits had been filed against my person. It was going to be hard to explain how a railway line two years in the planning had not yet broken a single shovelful of dirt, yet had taken many thousands of pounds sterling of the savings of tradesmen and lower-level government employees. I couldn't very well explain that the government itself had caused many problems with the laws it had passed.

At that point, Bellington resurfaced.

I expected him to move me back over into the business end of Bellington-Makepeace, to do accounting, as I had before, in case the elections didn't go off as planned.

We met in the disreputable tavern restaurant he loved so well. I hadn't even ordered a bowl of chowder before he spoke. "You're out as a candidate."

"If I lose, I lose. We're not the only ones taking a bath on this railroad collapse."

"I could let you stand for a vote, but you'd only be further humiliated. My associates and I have been giving the matter a lot of thought. The problem, son, is one of morality. Malfeasance. You own a railroad that never existed in the physical world. And now you're being called to account for it. Potentially it is a serious criminal offense."

"You bastard. This is the very thing I've tried to impress on you many times. I said the stock was overvalued. I begged you to get to work on the railroad. You said landowners had to be paid off first."

"That's all hindsight now. The pressing issue is your immediate situation."

"You dare speak to me of a situation? I wanted us to

become legitimate."

"Is that what you stand for? Acting in a legitimate manner? On all occasions?"

"I have no idea what you're talking about now."

"Don't you?"

He instructed me to take a prolonged vacation with Cecilia, to his country house in Ilfracombe, overlooking the very port that gave ships to King John in the 13th century to help defeat Ireland.

"You used me, Kip. You set me up as a dummy so that your friends and you could get richer without any adverse legal consequences. I assumed most of the risk."

"Technically that's true about the risk, but let's remain calm. Exactly for times like these I have in my employ two good solicitors."

"The ones who lost your big case?"

"Someone was bound to discover that lurking point of the law sooner or later. It just happened to be you."

"I don't understand how your businesses are so profitable, if this is how you think."

"That is the great secret, isn't it? We'll push through. Legions of defrauded customers are up in arms."

"Everybody wants to sue everybody. The very members of Parliament who created the mess with their excessive law making have lost vast sums of money, and some of them will doubtless lose their seats over this flap. Inquiries are happening, some of them led by the perpetrators. But we're more insulated than most. I have many business concerns, this being only the latest one. And in the current environment, there are plenty of places to scapegoat and share the blame."

"As you did with me?"

"Precisely. So, just you rely on me."

"Meaning?"

"We'll find a way to move you back over to the shipping side, over time. I'm afraid no matter what you're a bit exposed, as the company was yours in title. I made that pretty clear when you signed on. I need to think over how you fit with Bellington-Makepeace. But I'll give you an allowance in the meantime."

"Allowance?"

"Yes, I won't let you go hungry. The house you're renting may have to be let go, but you are the husband of my daughter, so it wouldn't be right to just leave you on the street."

"I have no wish to be patronized. I have money leftover from the stocks I sold, even if it was at a loss."

"Yes, dear fellow. I'm afraid that we're going to have to garnish that money for your legal fees. They are likely to add up, and I don't want to see you in prison because we couldn't afford to put up a good legal defense."

"Are you threatening me?"

"Goodness Kilcairn, you are quite the hothead. You're going to have to leave the solution to good old Kip, rely on his generosity, as head of the family, to get to the other side of this colossal mess."

"That means we'll be sharing again the residence on Warwick Street?"

Kip took me hard by the arm and pulled me close enough that I smelled the tobacco and beef, the curdled cheese and the bilge, on his breath. His eyes were bloodshot with weeks of spleen, years of bile, the acid borne of knowledge and ignorance mixed together like gin and tonic. "You haven't seemed to mind sharing what is in my house up until now. Have you?" He let the silence deepen around his words. "So why should that change? All this trouble has been a shock to my daughter. She's going to find out today that you will no longer be able to fulfill her dream of serving as a Member of Parliament. Her delicate state after the inevitable shock is all the more reason for Cecilia to have a good long rest. The two of you lay low on the shores of Ilfracombe and rest until you're summoned. I recommended long swims in the salt sea. Their waters are healing. Just try not to drown."

One afternoon I sat at the kitchen table painting a picture of the autumn leaves out the window, umber, burnt orange, yellow and brown, touched with frost, using the set of oil paints my mother had given me for my birthday, the best gift I'd ever received. She was making spoon bread, using a wooden cook spoon to measure out the dollops, to place on the wooden tray that would go into the kiln my father had built. I became excited with the prospect of the heat and taste of corn on my tongue, grabbing the little muffins off the tray as soon as she pulled it from the fire, burning my fingertips as she pretended to scold me while watching me gobble them up. I saw how busy she was with her recipe, but I hoped that she would turn around long enough to compliment me on the painting I had in progress.

Turn she did, suddenly absorbed in my work. With her free hand, she put her fingers on the discrete, wet brush strokes I'd applied, smearing them slowly, one might say methodically, so that the colors blurred, no longer resembling the leaves outside. "That's what it looks like in here," she said under her breath. I thought she was referring to the oven, but soon realized it wasn't that. Setting the spoon on the counter, she walked to the pantry door and began to beat her head against it in a slow repetition, as if she were playing a bodhran, except that the bodhran was herself. By the time my father came into the kitchen, drawn by her screams, her forehead was slathered in blood. I sat cowering in the corner, and when he'd taken her down the hallway to her room and shut the door, he had to climb under the table to pull me out.

It would make for a grim homily to say that I stopped painting—I did not. On the contrary, for a time, I painted more. I changed my style to the one she taught me that day, painting with my fingers, so that a red and green swirl with a thumbprint in the middle served as a man's head.

How to describe Ilfracombe? Hills lie upon hills, without visible valleys, so the land might as well be the waves of the sea, except that houses are piled upon them. The dwellings are gray, factory-like, their lines mean, except when the afternoon sun hits them right. Bellington's country house overlooked the town, its ugly vast terrace hanging to a hillside. But as you stand on the Tors, beneath lies the magnificence of the shore, its precipitous walls and battlements of rock fronting the bay—clay-slate, streaks of quartz, the gull's piteous cry, but no sand on which to sit and ponder. There was no place for Cecilia and me to take a moonlit wander and dissipate her sorrow of political loss out to the horizon. Our one attempt to clamber down to gather mollusks ended with cut hands.

Instead, we bought shellfish from the locals, cracked and cooked it. All we wanted was to be left alone. The reality of London vanished, to the point where we felt safe even as a gale beat the cliffs and forced us indoors. We found two bottles of white wine in the cellar. Cecilia and I made love, tender but not fragile. Each slow caress took us deeper into one another's attention. Her pale skin matched the ceaseless rain of that night, the very rain I'd always hated in Ireland, but now it washed the roof with a drowsy and comforting rhythm. We dozed until Cecilia jerked awake. I sat up, expecting one of her shrieks of old. All she did was light a candle and say, "There's something sad in the fugitive keenness of pleasure."

"Did you read that somewhere? Or was it born in sleep?"

"I don't know. It has lodged in my mind, no matter how it got there. Once my father took me down to the shore, at low tide, and we discovered a crass in a shallow pool. It had drawn in its tentacles, and covered itself with stones, mud and mucus. When it opened, white tentacles unfurled around a purple disc. It looked like a child's make-believe sun."

"I'm glad you have something pleasant to remember from those days."

"And what about you?"

"Well, my father—he gave me a book with uncut pages and a letter opener. I guess some friend had passed it onto him, and neither man read philosophy."

"You read it?"

"I did. It was Descartes' *Meditations.* That day marked the beginning of my education. I crawled under the table and sliced the first few pages open, as if I'd received a long-awaited letter from a friend. I understood nothing of its words at the time. The most I could do was commit some of its passages to memory, as if studying for a spelling contest. 'All that I have, up to this moment, accepted as possessed of the highest truth and certainty, I received either from or through the senses. I observed, however, that these sometimes misled us; and it is the part of prudence not to place absolute confidence in that by which we have even once been deceived.'

"I ran out the back porch and paced the dooryard, unreasonably excited. I ran my hands over an orange fungus that had grown on a neglected gatepost. Hoar frost covered the surface of an empty feeding trough. I heard my mother's eternally plaintive voice calling me to yet another dinner of bland mutton and I raced as far from the house as I could."

"And then?"

"Nothing, really. I stayed outdoors as long as possible, while a single star winked, and listened to the sheep bawl in their pens, as if they really had something important to relate. Finally, I went back inside. My father grumbled about me not helping him pen the animals. I didn't mention the book, which he'd forgotten about by then, because I knew he'd take it away, claiming that it distracted my mind from more important things."

In the morning, the gale having passed, we dried off a table and chairs on the balcony to sit and watch sea gulls crowd the shoreline rocks. Cecilia served fried fish with runny eggs and baguette slices. I took her hand in mine.

"I'm sorry you won't become a politician's wife."

"Don't worry. Maybe you'll stand at the next elections, once all this grousing about the railroads passes. Daddy is stubborn and doesn't tend to give up on things. That's how he made his millions. Why do we need so many railroads anyway? We got along fine without them before."

"I don't believe that electoral door remains open any longer. I may have to face a civil trial or a criminal one for defrauding investors."

"So what? You'll be vindicated. Answer me this: did you intentionally cheat those people out of their money?"

"No."

"Did you put your own earnings into this same venture, losing much of it in the panic?"

"Yes."

"Did you tell my father several times that he needed to get going on building the lines and the stations?"

"Yes."

"Did you on more than one occasion emphasize to him that the stock was highly overvalued, almost predicting that it would crash sooner or later?"

"Yes."

"And is it not the case that the government, from the Prime Minister all the way down, has been enabling this very situation by passing bad laws, based on wrong information, bribes, shameful self-interest, and deliberate deception, because each and every one of them thought he would make a personal fortune?"

"That is the truth."

"If anyone should be imprisoned, it's Kip Bellington. He has all the might, holds most of the cards, and is very good at manipulating people's minds and emotions. He knew exactly what he was getting into, and deliberately chose to make you the responsible party should things go wrong. I know I shouldn't say that about my own father, and of course I don't want him to go to prison either, and I doubt that he will. He's too smart and shifty and he has too many political friends. But if it comes to a choice between visiting my husband or father in prison, why I'll make Mister Bellington a nice pecan cake and read the newspaper to him in his cell on Sundays. Besides which, he owns part of a prison, so it would be just like living in his own house. God knows he doesn't want to inhabit the one on Warwick Street."

These were the most forceful words I had ever heard Cecilia speak at once, except for the night she told me about Wilberforce the cadet. I was astounded by her clear insight, her awareness, and her succinct analysis of everything that had just happened. No orator nor solicitor nor any statesman could have given such an eloquent discourse without a single word wasted.

"You might as well be my attorney," I told her. "It would keep him out of my savings a little longer."

"I'm not stupid, dear husband. I have spent much time listening to other people talk while they ignore me. I've heard Daddy go on endlessly about these matters, never soliciting my opinion, and you have come home several times complaining about these injustices to me and to the walls. I drew my own conclusions a long time ago. I would have told you to sell sooner, but I didn't want to interfere. Men are used to women being one more footstool to walk around or put their feet on. It's easier for the most part just to let the men have their way. Besides, I'm not strong like you, Kilcairn. You and my father are overpowering forces, you with your keen intellect and him with his smaller but iron mind bent on dominating everything around him. My mother too is a force of nature. I used to dream that I was a rabbit and that she held me in her hands, eating me alive while she ripped my fur apart with sharp fingernails. I would awake and expect to find her bloody fingerprints all over me. It's all I can do to stay alive in this world, to live through each day."

I began to cry. The noise I made was ugly, heinous and I gagged trying to get it out of me, like a black disease. The story of Priscilla and me locked together like two jackals spitting, biting, swallowing one another's saliva, tried to force its way through the small aperture of my throat. "There's something I have to tell you, Cecilia. Acts I'm not proud of."

She put her fingers to my lips. "You're a man, and you have certain needs I couldn't meet. It's biology and would be supported by the latest science, no doubt. You rented that apartment so you could have prostitutes when you needed them. They did for you the things I wasn't able to stand. They served as receptacles for an unspoken grief. Maybe it was for the best. I hope you won't need them now."

"Who told you that about me?"

"Let's put it behind us."

I had no idea what to respond. I could make up the existence of another woman, a lover, but that would be yet another lie told, not an improvement. "I'm sorry for what I did. I won't do it ever again."

"Then let's go hike on the Tors. The view from there is spectacular, the green and the blue. After last night's gale, the ocean from that great height is bound to look peaceful."

On hands and knees, Cecilia scrubbed the kitchen floor of her father's vacation home. I hadn't ever seen her so intent on labor. The bristles on the brush were old, half-spent, so it had no real effect on the grout. The size of the house was far beyond what two people might need, better suited for the gathering of a large extended family. I wondered what had possessed Bellington to buy it. Despite the expensive furnishings, the dank walls had sprouted a thin layer of mold, its faint scent hanging in the air. The kitchen floor had gone slick with coastal slime and each of us took a turn stumbling and almost falling.

"Let me help," I said, kneeling behind her.

Cecilia hurled the brush at the wall and it made a smack. "Whether you scrub or I do will make no difference. Why can't we return to London? We've been put in exile by a mad king. First they would hardly let us leave Warrick Street, and now they can't get us far enough away."

"Let's relocate somewhere. What's keeping us here besides the threat of me going to jail?"

"Don't joke with me, husband. If I had laudanum with me, I'd take it right now."

"Don't say that. You left it behind forever." I pulled her close where we sat on the grimy floor. "Would you ever consider living in Ireland?"

"Is that a serious proposal?"

"I never liked the countryside much. I've never told you this, but I grew up farming sheep. I don't want to return to that, but the Western coast is wild and gorgeous, just like this. Galway town has money and I could start a law practice there, with no one to chide us about bankruptcy."

"Yes! Of course, I would go."

"Then let me go first to visit my parents. I haven't seen them in several years."

"I didn't know you had parents. You never spoke of them, so I assumed they were dead. I want to accompany you. I want to meet them."

"Please, let me venture there first. I don't know in what state I'll find them, or how they'll receive me. It could be brutal. It won't be a happy reunion, of that I assure you. Then we'll travel back soon, together, to Galway, to see what prospects lie there. After that, I'll take you to meet my family, from a position of strength and security."

"Then I'll return to London."

"Couldn't you stay here until my return?"

"In a village where I know no one? No thanks. That's what you and I have a house for. You must trust me to know how to conduct myself around my parents."

"Of course, you do, my dear."

My arrival in Carickmannon to see my parents coincided with rain, as could be expected. For the first time since I was a child, the rolling fields looked velvety, beautiful, comforting, and I could say the word *emerald* without derision. I entered a tavern and ordered a small beer, as alcohol had never suited me, and now less than ever did I wish my wits muddled. The patroness, unfamiliar, looked at me as though I had asked for a plate of pus, and I settled for regular ale. No one on the premises seemed to recognize me, though I could see them squinting at this stranger, this interloper, trying to place him. Perhaps they all knew who I was and didn't want to comment. I had half hoped that Peggy might be tending the bar, so I could see how she looked now, whether she walked with a limp, or whether all signs of her injury had passed. I wouldn't put it past the farmers to jump on me in a pile and beat the living hell out of me, exacting revenge for the time I'd hurt her. I neither would have blamed them, nor protested. Yet not a word was exchanged, and I walked out untouched and unremarked.

I walked the mile, lugging a bag and an open umbrella, stepping around puddles as much as I could, but still getting flecks of mud on my shoes, as when I'd traversed the wet-spattered street leading to the Bingham Hotel right before I'd lain with Cynthia. There, beyond the repaired gate where my father let fly an expletive when I asked whether Jesus might revive my dead cat, sat the house, the same except that it was more weather-beaten, some stones half dislodged, the wood in need of a whitewash, and the roof of thatch sagging in places. My father had always kept it impeccable. I knocked at the door and Pa answered, saying nothing, waiting for me to speak first.

"I'm back, Pa."

"What for?"

"A visit, that's all."

He stepped aside and let me through, as though he didn't want my arm to brush his. The same workmanlike table, chairs, sideboard, hooked rug, and dark green draperies were there; nothing had changed. We'd never gone for anything fancy in our household. A sturdy piece of furniture would suffice, as long as it was kept in good repair. A cross hung over every lintel. A log burned in the fire, steady, as though it would never be consumed, but it didn't make the room any warmer.

"I'll get your mother."

He disappeared down the hall, and I stood, dripping umbrella in hand, not walking any further indoors, though it was the house in which I'd grown up. Soon my mother appeared. Her hairstyle hadn't changed, only some strands of gray had invaded her deep chestnut locks, and her forehead had taken on a small but permanent crease. She ran and flung her arms around my torso, hugging me long and hard, as though no one had touched her since I left. When she began to sob, I parted her from me gently, while my father looked away.

"I haven't made anything for supper. You should have told us you were coming. I've a pot roast left over from yesterday, and half a loaf of soda bread. There are apple conserves in the pantry."

"That will be plenty, Mum."

"You look handsome, son. As though you'd made something of yourself. Did it go well for you after all?"

I took off my soaked greatcoat, draped it over a chair to let it steam by the fire, and sat in the kitchen, as was our habit, while she sliced the cold roast and served me warm cider she'd drained from a bottle. After lingering in the doorframe, undecided whether to retire to his tick, I suppose, my dad pulled out a chair at the other end, letting it scrape the floor, which no longer had much varnish to its boards.

"How have you been?"

Pa peered at me from beneath whitish brows. "What do you care?"

"Cioran, please let the boy speak his piece." The vicious tone of old in her was absent; I would have described her as polite, as though my father were an acquaintance not accustomed to loud talk.

"Things went quite brilliantly for a time. I married well, into one of the top families in London, and became a candidate for Parliament. I worked for a shipping company, as their accountant." Of the railroad I planned to say nothing. Whether or not my father had read the right newspapers, and the news had reached him, he wasn't going to mention.

"That's lovely, son. I knew you'd make us proud."

"Proud?" Pa stood up, looking every bit of his six feet in height, still rugged. "He didn't invite us to his wedding. This is the first we know of Kilcairn having a wife. I don't suppose it would have suited his pretense to show off a couple of rude peasants such as us. King Herod was never so mortified of the beaten Christ."

"Maybe you can take us with you now, son. I'd love to meet that wife of yours and the rest of the company you keep. Why didn't you bring her?"

"What, woman? You want to go as her lady in waiting? I guess Kilcairn can lend us a servant's quarters at the back of his house."

"I know I didn't treat you and Mum as I should have. I'm going to pay back all of what you gave me."

"You think I want your money? I suppose this farm looks disheveled to you now, but we haven't reached rack and ruin, nor will we. What I could have used were your hands, to rebuild the pens and the barn, to mow the hay, to cut wood for the fire. I've only so much mortal strength. But I've made do with my own back and arms, and the help of a lad or two in town who wasn't so stuck up. Have you cuffed other girls as you did Peggy?"

"That was a long time ago, husband. It happened only once, and I'm sure he's regretted it plenty since."

"Let the randy goat speak for himself."

"You're right, Pa. What I did was wrong. And I've a conscience. I went to the tavern first to find Peggy and to apologize."

"You needn't waste your time looking. She removed to County Cork with her husband; a veterinarian and they've a child. You're not the only native son who made good."

To my surprise, I remained calm. I was glad I hadn't brought Cecilia. "I'd be happy to have you come to London with me, except that Cecilia and I plan to return to Ireland."

My mother set down a spoon. "To Carickmannon? No one in the village needs a solicitor, not much. They only stand before a county judge and state their case, and that's all there is to it."

"Not here. Perhaps we'll set up house in Galway. We'll visit again soon, with your blessing, and venture on to the western coast to see whether we might find luck."

My father stood up and flung a chair at a wall, not hard, but deliberately, enough to command my attention. "As far as I'm concerned, I have no desire to ever see you again. If you come, give me advance notice. Find what lodging you can in town. If you need a few shillings, I'll search in a drawer."

I looked to my mother for any opposing word, but she uttered none. The sprite had gone out of her, the demon too, and all that remained was a gaunt woman of straw in a checked frock.

Part II

The crossing of the Irish Sea offered smooth slate water, as if to speed my return from Ilfracombe and back to Cecilia. London welcomed me with a teal sky and many partridges cooing in trees along the way. I arrived at a vacant house. I drifted though rooms, noticing a light dust on a bookcase. There was nothing to do except hire a carriage over to Warwick Street. When I rang, the hired girl opened after a short wait.

Priscilla sat at a desk in the parlor. Only a glance met mine, and she went back to her task. "I suppose you're looking for Cecilia. You shan't find her here, or at your home either."

"Where, pray tell, might I encounter her?"

"Kip will be along in about an hour. As I understand, the two of you have unfinished business. In the meantime, I have a game of whist to make."

Whist? She stepped around me, gathered her purse, a black hat of fine woven straw and a leather band, and left the house without any further word. The hired girl didn't appear nor offer any tea until I called out and asked for it. The afternoon light in the high windows went from salmon to blue before a step was heard and Kip came into view round the corner, eating a sugar cookie. I would describe him as a man who had recently been angry, the incipient dissipation of ire still beaded on his skin.

He plopped down in the chair opposite me, as though we were about to drink sherry, like we had on my first visit to the house. But there was no sherry in sight. "You fucked my wife."

"Excuse me?"

"I won't excuse you. Don't try to deny it. I've given great thought to the matter. I don't want a scandal. Cecilia knows what you did to Priscilla. The bruise marks, the choking, all that. I don't want to make you a martyr for her sake. She is rather sentimental and might even hold it against me. I'd rather let her be guided by her own blind fury, which right now is considerable. She was skeptical at first, but no one except the most demented individual could make up a story like that, not even my wife."

"You knew what was going on between Priscilla and me. You tolerated it because I had more value to you as a shill."

"A suspicion and a fact are not the same."

"If Priscilla ended up in my arms, it was because she couldn't tolerate you."

"Perhaps you're right. However, things have become quite cozy between us. I gave up my apartment across town. You've done us a favor, Kilcairn. Without meaning to, you've set our marriage to rights by expanding our horizons. Whether I prove as adept as you I can't yet say, but I am trying."

"I insist on speaking to Cecilia."

"Don't worry. I'll send her around to you tomorrow, if that's what you really wish. I only wanted us to talk first, like two gentlemen. Speak your piece with my daughter. I have confidence she'll make the right decision. We were a family long before you came on the scene, and so we shall continue."

"Cecilia is my wife."

"Legally, yes, but no longer in spirit. That is why I am asking you to divorce her. Certainly we can make things nasty in court and revive your recent reputation as someone untrustworthy. We have all those defrauded investors who could be used as character witnesses. Priscilla is ready to testify that you raped her. The housekeeper is willing to swear that she caught you coming out of my wife's room, just before she emerged, battered and bruised. I located a prostitute, or bribed one, I can't remember which, who is willing to swear that you have violent, sociopathic tendencies. And so on. This is what I suggest. I will pay you a reasonable settlement so that you can get your own business or law practice started, whatever it is you want to do."

"You mean return the profits from the stock shares you took away."

"In return, you agree to a clean divorce, move to a neighborhood far from here, and never see her or us again. Or you can spend a long time in prison. I own part of one—I'm not sure whether Cecilia ever mentioned that."

"I don't want your money."

"Suit yourself. I've already deposited it to your account, for services rendered to Bellington and Makepeace. A severance is what I called it in the books. Do with it what you want. Burn it. Or better yet, give it the poor. That's a passion of yours, isn't it, bleeding for the underserved? I'm not sure what Irish sheep farmers usually do when they come into money."

I hurried down the brick steps. A few days later, Cecilia sent a note stating that she had no intention of seeing me. My many attempts to contact her were in vain. She traveled to France, the specific destination unknown to me, where she stayed for months, safely out of my reach.

Part III
DEIRDRE

It was lucky that I hadn't stood for Parliament. Without meaning to, Bellington had done me a favor by yanking me as a candidate, and I had really ceased to think of him at all. None of the lawsuits filed against me had ever gone forward, as I had no real means with which to pay settlements, and so solicitors left me alone. I have no idea what lawsuits Bellington ended up in. He was always embroiled in lawsuits anyway, and usually he won them. In any case, when I began to work as an attorney, judges treated me with the usual slight disparagement afforded to most of our kind, nothing better, but nothing worse.

It would have been far better for me had I simply been banished outright from polite company. In a sense I was, but not by any official edict. I'd thought the world in general, men of prestige, would have come down on me hard. Yet I was not ejected from the Oxford-Cambridge club. No one invited me to their houses or approached me with offers of employment, nor were they openly derisive. I could feel mute sympathy in the circumspect faces of some. They all knew they could have been crushed in the hand of Bellington. They saw me as an object lesson in not drawing too near to his company. They hated him, yet many were obliged to do business with him. Lord Houghton paved the way for me at the club, I think. He knew I needed a refuge.

I fantasized about harming Bellington, but if I failed, I would be subjected a second time to his crushing wrath. He held all the cards. In a sense I didn't care, as many a morning I awoke with the thought of no longer wanting to live, a passive desire to dissolve. I couldn't expose myself to the possibility of failure, should I fail to fell him with a pistol shot. I didn't want to be a coward either, assaulting by surprise, but there could be no chance of a duel. If there had, I would have taken my chances, with the consolation of killing or being killed, on some remote plain where the railroads were to have been built, our seconds there to vouch that all had been done with honor. I would go out a gentleman or remain as a victor. I saw no way out, and my discomfort at the club grew as members welcomed with hearty, artificial handshakes, an object of pity.

Lord Houghton, tired of my despondence, got me invited to an autumn ball. I demurred, but he had produced for me an enchanting sylph from an Irish family of some repute, one without prejudice who genuinely seemed to like me. As I did a serviceable Mazurka, I began to notice the simpers of some of the assembled ladies, looking at me. I was nobody. They had nothing to lose by their rude stares. My date, embarrassed, made an excuse that she had come down with "pallor," and excused herself. As I walked to a waiting tray of Scotch, I heard a woman say, "Serves him right." "Arriviste," agreed another. "You can dress up a monkey, but you can't hide what you are."

I would have taken a bust and knocked both unconscious had I been able. I also made excuses to Lord Houghton. I began to notice the same behavior from women in the street as I passed, especially lower-class women, even prostitutes along the quay. People were defiling Cecilia's name indirectly with their vicious gossip. I literally wanted to kill someone—specific persons, but really anyone. But I knew this fantasy was beneath me.

Within three months I had a law practice going, small but solvent. One morning a widow came into my law office wearing a trim woven hat, slender fingers held out to greet me, one glove removed. She'd heard I was an attorney for remaindered people.

"You don't look remaindered," I said. "You look—unfinished." It's extraordinary how a woman's diction and elocution can move me.

Deirdre wore a black sheath dress high at the neck, one that, paradoxically, wouldn't have been acceptable in Priscilla's cleavage-baring crowd, who wrap themselves in abundant pricey cloth, yet forget to cover the parts that want to be looked at. That same week, I had strangled a young woman. The image of the flower girl still stayed vivid within me. I had carried her to the river on my shoulders, wrapped in a sheet I sewed into a bag, and dumped her, not knowing what else to do. A single person could have stopped me, yet no one did. I should have gone to prison, and everything else would have followed from that.

As I weighed her body down by placing rocks inside the bag, as in my dream, and watched her sink, it came back to me, what I might call a brusque reverie, that no best friend had drowned me. My father had once "taught" me to swim by carrying me on his massive shoulders out into the pond water, and dropping me summarily into its relative depths.

I told myself that strangling the flower girl had been simply an impulse. There was no sense going into reasons. The important thing was that it would not happen again.

Is it strange that the fact of a lady removing one glove while keeping the other on was enough to provoke my rapt attention? She took my hand, a gesture that made me flinch. I wanted no one to stir my senses. The violence in me had quelled, or had it? It might simply have represented an impulse never to be repeated. The ache of Cecilia's absence stirred still in me, not the beautiful sorrow of poets, not Byron's "She walks in beauty, like the night/of cloudless climes and starry skies," but rather more like an infected tooth and any poke made it swell and redden.

"How may I help you?"

"It's about a will."

"A grandparent?"

"No, my recently deceased husband. It's not so much. But a cousin has appeared, very insistent and with a wily barrister. I really don't have the cash to retain a good one."

"So you came to me."

"That's not what I meant. Everybody says you're the best of the younger men, new, hungry, ethical, and that you're confident enough of your skills to decide which cases to take."

"They said all that?"

"It's the impression I took."

I didn't contradict her directly that in fact I took on every case I could garner. Her expression of quiet sorrow was like clouds that lower over the city for hours without ever turning to rain. "I appreciate the flattery. But I wouldn't exaggerate my prowess. I do the best I can with the clientele I'm given."

"I'd rather have him back than the money; do you understand? Only I don't have that choice."

"I'll take your case."

"But I haven't told you the particulars."

"It doesn't matter. I'll win it or I won't."

I won it, in fact. It took two weeks. The amount in dispute was quite substantial. The cousin's lawyer acted aggressive by nature, used to winning, but I could tell he was unnerved by me. It was as though the smell of the flower girl still clung to my skin, the wilted petals right at the point between pungently fragrant and rotten. As I walked the streets, it was as though I were in a parade or a coronation, in which those who thronged the streets tossed flower petals before my step, with knowing eyes. Before the judge, I was quiet, deliberately sly, as though there were much more I could tell, if I'd wanted. My words were few and my pauses were long.

I made quite a bit of money off that case, more than I had since I'd set up a practice. Deirdre wanted to celebrate this victory of her new widowhood by cooking me goulash. Her grandparents were Hungarian immigrants and had left her with that palate for a cheap cut of meat, slow stewed and seasoned with paprika. It reminded me that I hadn't always dined on the softest flesh.

"You've really repaid me more than enough with my fee."

"The matter goes beyond money." She took my hand and I didn't pull away.

"Then I accept. I don't mean to sound ungrateful."

"That's more like it, then. Tomorrow night. You know my address from the documents I signed."

"Just me?"

"Did you want a chaperone?"

"No, of course not."

"Kilcairn—may I now call you by your first name? And you can call me Deirdre."

"Well then, I'll see you again soon." She kissed me on the cheek, giving off a whiff of oleander.

A hard rain battered my house that night. I had purchased a bottle of rum, but when I opened it, the fragrance was cloying. I sweated, even with the windows open and gusts of rain leaving puddles on the sills. There was still time to call off the impending dinner.

The cleaning woman had waxed my floorboards. They gleamed with the sheen one finds on the surface of a lake in the proper light. If I slipped and hurt myself, I'd have a good excuse for begging off from the dinner. I removed my shoes and walked across the room in my sock feet. I didn't even slide.

I lay on my bed and masturbated, an act I rarely do, even during celibate periods, as the idea of producing my own effluence disgusts me. My mind began to swarm with fevered images of the Widow Waller, her dress ripped from her shoulders, her skin covered in soot. Or perhaps they were bruises. Soon I had her on hands and knees waxing my floor, while I knelt and attacked her from behind. I worked my way up and down the social scale: fishwife, spouse of the Minister of Justice, laundress come to wash my sheets, rider in a steeplechase bent over a saddle. These images should have made me burst out laughing, yet they led me, with excruciating slowness, to a climax, during which I yelled as if someone had stolen my wallet and was running off down the street.

This exercise only made me feel worse. I decided to walk to the home of the Widow Waller and make excuses for not being able to attend her intimate soirée. I plunged into the torrent outside without an overcoat or umbrella, and at once the rapid rain saturated my clothes. I had walked five or six blocks of the twenty that separated us before I turned around.

During dinner the next day, instead of contemplating the graceful curves filling Deirdre's teal blouse, I'd think on the shock and awe of the gallows, as once upon a time in the schoolhouse, to keep myself in check. I arrived home, shed my wet clothes and lay on the bed again, not even bothering to towel myself dry. I remained supine like malarial Saint Teresa, the patroness of headache sufferers. Without a blanket, I lay waiting for a willing fever to descend, but all I got for my trouble was a sleepless night of chattering teeth. My constitution is simply too strong, like that of my father, who gets up each morning to herd the rams and ewes, no matter the weather.

I set out for Deirdre's to supper, now under an empty blue sky, vowing not to bring any item that could be misconstrued as encouragement of a further liaison between us. Yet despite myself I bought a bouquet of flowers for my client, trapped in the sense of decorum I had spent years instilling in myself. To make matters worse, I picked up a bottle of wine, which she would end up drinking while I abstained, making her entirely vulnerable.

I knocked on her door and she answered. Behind her hung the fragrance of the slow-stewed beef, the promised goulash. As soon as the door closed, she snuggled against my front and gave me a deep kiss. My arms hung helpless, a bottle in one hand and dahlias in the other. She undressed me as if she were looking for a brooch I'd filched off her person, one she wanted back badly. "I've been waiting a long time for this opportunity."

"Opportunity? What a strange word."

"It's precisely what I meant to say." We sank onto the nearby settee and she explored my skin with her mouth and hands, without disrobing. "My dead husband was a great lover. He kept me satisfied for ten years before a heart attack took him. And since he died, seven weeks ago, I've had no hand to touch me, no man's body to please and to have his please me. We'll have goulash later."

I wanted to reach out with a jerk and watch a bone button fly. But I made myself remove her blouse and skirt slowly, unhook her brassiere with care, after which my hands slid under her breasts, feeling their weight, their sheer reality. I helped her lie back on the carpet and slid into her without hurrying, feeling myself enveloped, concentrating on the sensation of warmth, experiencing a friendly encounter, wholesome, natural, the thing mammals do to feel safe within the general terror that is the world. This is how children are made, how the species perpetuates and animates the clay that sometimes goes by the name of kindness. I tried to will my mind blank, the way lovers do, but I couldn't help wonder what were the exact physical habits with which she'd greeted her husband, developing over time, instinctual and sure, until they became a routine, that place between comfort and wild excitement, the skill of repeating what works replacing novelty.

"Hold my wrists behind my head."

"Is that how he did it? Your dead husband?"

Instead of slapping me as I deserved, she breathed, "Yes. That's how I like it."

Part III

It was the most placid romantic encounter with a woman that I'd ever had. Sex with Cecilia had mostly been healthy, affectionate, but always with a slight anguish behind, the sense that the frieze would crack, and the god and goddess would fall to the floor in pieces. I had considered the waxy melting of legend just that, a metaphor to give us hope. But here it was. Afterward, Deirdre stroked the back of my head as she kissed my damp locks.

"You gave me just what I needed," she said.

A widow's fee from Deirdre should have sufficed, and if not, a quick celebratory toss, goulash, and a discreet farewell. Deirdre slept long, and I enjoyed how the soft light only a candle can lend surrounded her face. I imagined her dead, in repose exactly like this, no marks on her throat, no blade having invaded her side, no thought of kidneys or gristle or guts.

She'd drunk the entire bottle of wine I'd bought and stumbled to her chamber with clumsy limbs. The only sign she had left of her husband was a cameo on the mantelpiece. Pushing away the embrace of her fingers, I slid out of bed, went to the cameo and held it before me. I wanted to hurl the cameo against the wall, hear it splinter, awaken Deirdre and watch her cry as she knelt over the fragments, trying to piece them together. Instead, gently, I set down his portrait and slipped back into bed. Turning on her side, she brought her mouth to my chest, still half asleep, and licked at my nipple the way a cat breaks the skein on a dish of cream.

I grabbed her train of hair, fastened at the back, and jerked it. Deirdre cried out. I entered her with force, pressing her torso close to mine, hands held tightly to her back, crushing her, not leaving a centimeter of space between us as I rolled on top of her belly and chest. "You're suffocating me," she protested, trying in vain to push my weight off hers. As we struggled and she scratched at my neck, she began to shudder until she simply went limp. I let her go and sat up, as did she.

"What the hell was that?"

"Didn't you want me to please you?"

"I'm not sure I'd call what just happened pleasure."

"Then why did you like it?"

"It's a good question. Jasper never did such a thing to me. If he had I would have slapped him."

"You didn't slap me."

"Just shut up, please." Still fuming, she turned up the lamp, sat naked at the dining table with legs splayed, and spread marmalade on a leftover piece of toasted bread. Deirdre took a large bite, rubbed a dollop from her lip with her wrist, and chewed with her mouth open. Her body was robbed of every speck of erotic appeal. She might as well have been a base mammal squatting in a cave. Yet that mammal sat alone, and I wasn't going to abandon her in the middle of the night.

She offered me nothing to eat. I waited for her to finish her toast, drink a glass of water, and told her to come back to bed so we could get some rest. Gingerly, she returned and lay down again. "No more tonight. That's as far as we go."

"I understand. I'm not a savage."

"That's a matter of opinion."

How quickly we pass from that ecstatic plane of expectancy into the terrain of what is familiar, with its gripes and grumbles. I'd hoped to end the evening on a note of restrained nobility. "Of course, beloved."

She smirked at the word beloved. "Let's not get carried away." Turning her back to me, Deirdre got into a comfortable position. "It's best that I not be seen going out of the house with my solicitor. I'd prefer that you leave either before cockcrow, so as not to be spotted, or at midday, when it would be normal for a solicitor to be visiting on business."

"Now that you've received the service you wanted."

"I suppose so. If that's what you want to call your mauling."

After tossing and turning for an hour, I got up, donning my clothes and pulling on my boots. I left her bedroom and walked the streets for hours, listening to the creak of branches until the clangor of the garbage man's bells announced the arrival of day.

A drip in the ceiling of my law office would not go away. No matter how busy I kept myself building the practice, my thoughts would turn to Cecilia, and I would wonder whether she had returned to London or was still ensconced in France living the life of a wronged heroine who doesn't even get her own novel. I had called for a workman to stop the drip, but in suddenly leaky London, none was available until the following day. In that state of vexation, I closed the office and walked to the house of Deirdre, paying no mind to the larkspur that wanted to pull me out of my bad mood with its practiced trills. The widow and I hadn't spoken since the night I left abruptly. Had I been the mere accessory to a short-lived celebration of her recovered income before being given the boot from bed and heart? So it seemed. I wasn't happy at having my heart opened just when I'd fastened it neatly shut.

Though there was a bell to ring, I rapped on the door. Presently, Deirdre peeped out. "Kilcairn. I thought you were someone else. You can't be here."

"Am I interrupting something?"

"No, it's just I thought you were someone—that is, you're my attorney, and I'm going to need your professional advice soon. I'm being sued by a merchant about money Jasper apparently promised to pay. I was about to come see you myself on the morrow in your office."

"Ah, Jasper. He continues to give us common cause beyond the grave."

"Don't say it that way, Kilcairn. Jasper is my heart's loss, but your patron saint."

"Is that what he is? Well then, you might as well let me in so we can go over your business."

"That's more like it." She slid the chain. It was four in the afternoon, the safest hour of the day, according to police statistics. The men of the family are just returning from their sojourns, the wives or maids have supper on in a roasting pan, the lads and lasses from school are spending graphite and clay on paper to do their sums. The parish priest can be received for a quick proverb and cup of tea, so long as he washes his hands before he can be offered a slice of cake.

"On your way to Mass?"

"Yes, in fact. The girl has just—gone fifteen minutes ago."

I knew this not to be the case, by the unnecessary way she stuttered getting the sentence out. Someone, yes, had left fifteen minutes ago, and she must have thought he'd come back for his hat, only to find me instead on the stoop alongside the weather-beaded tulips.

"I've missed you," I said.

"Mourning is a delicate time. I hope you don't take it amiss that I'm in a hurry. I'm going to say a Mass for my husband."

"Again?"

"You can't say too many."

"Was his soul in peril?"

"No more than anyone's. But I can't be too careful. Sometimes I still hear him drifting along the corridor, as though he's waiting to be released."

"Those were my footsteps leaving your house."

"I apologize. I didn't mean to be dismissive. I just don't think it's a good idea for us to be seen together, except for business."

"I want to continue with you, Deirdre. I care about you very much. I didn't want to cross over from our professional relationship, but when you kissed me, I understood again what it feels like not to care about anything except the person in front of you."

"Goodness. All that from a kiss."

"I'm not asking you to marry me or be my fiancé. I know you've just been widowed. Is it too much for us to just have dinner together, talk, keep company?"

"The other night, you gave me—relief, but afterward, I felt nothing. You're not like him. All I'd ever do would be to find you wanting."

"I gave you relief? As from a cough?"

"I didn't mean it that way."

I began to pace, as the blood simmer rose within me. "William Gladstone may have a sentimental attachment to fallen women, but his father owned slaves in the West Indies. That was the first speech he made as a Tory MP—defending his father."

"What has Gladstone to do with anything?"

"Nothing, except it would be ironic if I ended up in servitude on one of his father's plantations."

"You? Transported? I thought that was for criminals. I don't like the look on your face. You seem very agitated."

"Precisely. Bellington had everything to do with Gladstone getting appointed to the Board of Trade. At the time I thought that man might be instrumental in my ascent. He told me in person that he thought I might make a wonderful Cabinet member someday, just like him. Only he doesn't like the Irish, as it turns out."

"I didn't know you were a politician."

"Yes, well, almost. You didn't read about me in the newspaper?"

"No, I'm sorry. I don't follow politics. They just said you were a good lawyer."

"Too bad. You might have found me more impressive had you known, except that I never had the chance to win."

"You are impressive. I didn't mean to imply otherwise."

"Ah, is that so? The Lunacy Commission recently restrained Gladstone's sister. According to them, she suffers chronic instability, a string of lovers, and worse still, opium addiction. The news pained me so much, I guess, because it reminded me of Cecilia. But you know what it was in the end?"

"I don't even know what you're talking about. Who is Cecilia?"

"She converted to Catholicism."

"Cecilia?"

"Gladstone's sister. Gladstone could tolerate all her other failings, but not apostasy." I grabbed the Widow Waller by the front of her dress. "You broke my heart, Deirdre."

She pushed me away. "Can't you take our encounter for what it was? I was in the throes of grief."

"The throes? That's dialogue from a bad play."

"I swear to God I was—we weren't—I was going to seek you out again."

"For advice."

"Not just that. I'm fond of you. I don't know what I want. You made me happy that day. I was grateful."

I had grasped her wrist, and with rough jerks I guided Deirdre into the dining room. I knew I had gone too far. I knew the best thing I could do was go sup at a tea shop nearby, where I could sit. Wanting to get away from me, she grasped the tablecloth and let out a shriek. Deirdre lurched and hit her head on the edge of the table. She fell to the floor with a groan and was silent.

The blow had not drawn blood, only caused an ugly swelling at one temple, which was quickly becoming purple. I found an ice pick and chipped enough slivers for a compress for her head. I held it there for several minutes, knowing that she was in fact already dead. I dragged her body to the bedroom and placed her on the bed. On an instinct, I slipped one hand under her skirt, touched between her legs with the tip of a pinky, drew it out to inspect and, just as I suspected, she was freshly wet and sticky inside.

Even when night fell, and it would have been prudent to leave, I lay beside her in bed for several hours. I had wanted to take her to the Lake District. Or we would hold hands while strolling past the tobacconist's shop, the grocer's, sitting at the foot of some famous statue that, however fouled by pigeons, managed to keep its dignity.

I kept vigil in her bedroom, with the lamp turned up as high as it would go; as I imagined that a rat might crawl from a space in the wall and disfigure her. When my aunt died in Carickmannon, my mother had left me alone in her farmhouse for just that reason, so the departed wouldn't be alone before the wake, when a rodent might invade the house. I was told to sit in the bed beside her, not to move from that spot until the aunties of the village came to dress her in austere calico and make her up for the funeral with the herbs and clays that only pointed up the fact that she'd soon pass to a state of dirt. As I hunched over my knees and clasped them, I felt my aunt shriveling beside me in the dark, hissing as her soul leaked from some hidden place.

I put on my topcoat and leather gloves and crept down the stair of Deirdre's home. I had no strength to make it all the way to my own apartment. Instead, I went straight to my office and curled in my desk chair until a policeman who still looked a boy woke me.

"Sir, I am sorry to disturb you. But one of your clients has been murdered."

"Who? I'm sorry, but I don't practice that kind of law."

"No, sir, you misunderstand. You're needed at the station for questioning."

"I worked half the night. I have deadlines. Now you're just going to put me further behind."

"I'm sure that's true sir. I doubt they'll keep you long. Our precinct captain is known for his efficiency."

Before long, I sat in a room with three interrogators who seemed none too friendly, and to whom my name apparently meant nothing. They shambled through an inept line of questioning leading nowhere, until the aforesaid captain entered, his uniform crisp as his syllables.

"You have a right to legal representation, like anybody."

"I'm an attorney, so I don't need another."

"I'll be succinct. You were seen a week ago to have emerged from the residence of the recently widowed Mrs. Waller at an unbecomingly late hour."

"Unbecoming? What exact hour is that?"

"Spare me your sarcasm. Between midnight and morn."

"In legal terms, that's not a very specific window. I remember nothing of the kind. I had dinner with her, and we parted. In any case, what has that to do with now?"

"Nothing, yet. It's just a circumstance. But did there exist some affectionate relationship between yourself and Mrs. Waller?"

"Money."

"Well, she's come to an unfortunate end. She received a nasty blow to the head, possibly from a jealous lover."

"Not that it's any of my business, but couldn't it have been a robbery?"

"Nothing got taken and no evidence could be found of a forced entry. It had to be someone she knew."

"She was my client and had pending a lawsuit from a local merchant. You can check on that story if you like. Our relationship was purely professional."

"Well, we have no other suspect at the moment. So the light shines on you unless someone comes up with a different idea."

"An idea?"

"What I mean is, they're just gathering evidence."

"I'll be going, unless you have another reason to detain me."

"Not for the moment. But remember you no longer have the protection of Kip Bellington. If you did do something to the Widow Waller, you'll pay for it. You should have won that seat in Parliament. Then you could kill whoever you want."

My worst fear is not death, but, beyond drowning, being put away under the power of another human, especially one base, ignorant, and unlikely to exercise any sense of self-control. Bellington had crushed me, I'd survived, and nobody else was going to get me under this thumb. "You speak of gathering evidence.

Did you check her for semen?"

"Excuse me?"

"You heard what I said."

"That's vulgar."

"To the squeamish. I mean no disrespect. I would like to help you solve the crime that took the life of an innocent woman. Dr. Baynard published a paper a full five years ago that established procedures for the microscopic detection of sperm. Is that news?"

"Is this the sort of thing you gentlemen discuss at the club while you eat rare beef and mashed potatoes?"

"She was seeing a man. I don't know his name, just that he visited her. There was some sort of trouble there, but nothing actionable. Volatile domestic passions are not my area of law. But the last time I was at her residence on business, he had left a few minutes before, so she said. She thought I was he, coming back for his hat, and she seemed fearful. He could have gone there last night. Check her for semen."

"I'll pass along your tip, just so they can understand how the mind of a pervert works. I expect I'll see you again."

"Good day, then."

"I can't say I wish you the same."

When the semen analysis had been completed, a Mr. Fisher was identified, an insurance man, based on descriptions of him by neighbors. He and Deirdre had been seen in a bakery, buying ginger snaps. As a material witness, I was simply asked to repeat what I had told the police. The police captain stood by with a sour look, now that his hasty accusation had been discredited. Or maybe he was just jealous that my police work turned out to be better than his.

Based on the identification of Mr. Fisher's sperm freshly within her, he looked set to be convicted of manslaughter and sentenced to ten or twenty years in prison. It was surmised that they'd had an amorous argument after intercourse and he'd pushed her, causing her to fall and strike her head. After the first day in court adjourned, I sat ignoring a beer in a nearby pub, considering how I had the power to set things straight and free Mr. Fisher by simply telling the truth about what had happened. Mrs. Waller had become agitated, slipped and knocked her head, dying almost instantly. Neither of us had killed her. It really was an accident. But my having placed her in the bed, failing to call the authorities, or to look for medical help, would put me in prison. I had no faith that justice could really be done. I couldn't sleep that night and attended the second day of the trial, pondering whether to come clean.

But I didn't have to say anything. Mr. Fisher's defense successfully argued that the state of scientific evidence remained in doubt. The forensic techniques being used were too new, too subject to interpretation, and the sample appeared too contaminated, possibly from my having reached in, for men of reason to concur on its origin. After all, he said in a final burst, it could have been anyone's! This sally provoked great laughter throughout the courtroom. The judge dismissed the case, and Mr. Fisher walked free. The litigious cousin ended up getting his money after all. The atmosphere of the courtroom at the end resembled that of a successful auction.

I knew that if I didn't get out of London immediately, I would kill someone very soon. A woman. Sometimes when I closed my eyes at night, I saw the faces of those so-called ladies at the ball whirling around me, or jerk awake from a dream that whores and shop girls lined the streets to mock me as I rode in a carriage, a parade of one, down a main boulevard.

The next day I closed the office and left for Cornwall. I knew nothing of that region, except that Merlin cast his first prophecies there, foreboding words about luxury, fornication, and the Baths of Badon running cold. But the impulse that drew me was a railroad slated to be built, one that might or might not run through there. Seven and ¼ broad gauge, over the expanse of the River Tamar, right where the Tamoaze Ferry crossed, propelled by a piston in a tube that would run between the two rails. It was going to cost £1,600,000, financed by a bloc of partners. Lord Houghton had invited me to dinner to discuss the fact that there was a struggle going on over whether the line was to be built via the central route, bypassing Cornwall, or the southern route, if the Great Western Railway could be persuaded to connect with the South Devon Line. The matter had been killed and revived in Parliament more than once.

Lord Houghton thought I had a significant role to play. He wasn't always taken quite seriously in Parliament, despite the fact that he was smarter than most of them. Yet he did have his allies. He was one of the few who hadn't rejected me after what happened. His attention wandered in a thousand places at the same time, and I think on the day he sent me an invitation, I just happened to lie at the other end of a simile that was forming in his mind. He was an inveterate prankster who, when I'd first known him, convinced me to buy a hippopotamus with him, one that would be delivered to us in a wagon. I, wary by nature, waited for a week before I realized

I'd been had. So I was flattered at the presumed confidence in me regarding this new proposition, yet I didn't take him quite at his word.

"Aren't the reformatories and copyright your pet causes, Houghton? Since when do you know anything about the railroads?"

"Don't underestimate my ability to get my fingers sticky, Kilcairn. If you're not interested in the offer, you might instead accompany me to Paris, where there is bound to be a bloody insurrection soon. Somebody has to write about it. I recognized at once that wounded expression you try to pass off as cynicism."

"I've worked in the blighted realm of railroads before," I told him. "And it's not somewhere I ever want to go again."

"But the money, man, the money."

"I took a horrible beating the first time around."

"What about revenge?"

"I'm surprised to hear you suggest that. You don't seem like the vengeful sort."

"We're not talking about me, Kilcairn. We're talking about you." He assured me he had given the matter a great deal of consideration before approaching me. I had managed a railroad on paper and had taken the time to learn the laws and technical aspects. I had beaten the Norwegians at the maritime legal game, a single-handed feat that would not soon be forgotten by those who were fair minded. If I could show a little charm, I might find myself in the midst of this route negotiation.

"Why me, Houghton? Everyone else has left me for dead. I can't even get a glance of contempt when I cross the path of anyone from that time."

"Perhaps it's because you're the only one who truly

appreciated my poem about flagellation."

"No one else I know can put so much comic pain into hexameters. And that's saying a lot coming from me, because my sense of humor is not the keenest."

"Don't you remember, good man, how Rousseau wondered by what sequence of miracles the strong came to submit and serve the weak?"

"And which am I, sir, in your railroad parable?"

"That's what I'd like to find out, Kilcairn. We won't know unless you secure an interview, with a letter of introduction from me, with Messieurs Tweedy and Bond, who have just written a prospectus for the Cornwall Railroad. They need an attorney with knowledge of railroads to close the deal with the GWR for the southern route. Their own are about to lose the deal, and a lot of money will fall to Bellington. These men know about you and are impressed. You ought to pay them a visit."

It sounded like another of Houghton's pranks, another hippopotamus for me to buy. I wasn't going to be gullible again. But on reflection, and after the sordid interlude with Deirdre and its fatal consequences, Houghton's overture made all the sense in the world. It was a chance I needed to take. I would never reach Kip's stature, wealth, or influence. But I could force him to read my name in the newspaper as I stood beside Tweedy, Bond, and the other investors, as one of them drove a railroad spike into the ground, as one does to rid the world of a vampire. I realized that in part I'd never considered making him vanish from the world because, however distant the hope, I wanted him to see me rise again, to know that he couldn't simply erase me. This was my chance.

Snow had been falling all week outside the courthouse and in the rest of the city, limning tree branches and mucking up the streets. The temperature had dropped, as quickly as a bird that dies in mid-air as the atmosphere takes on the first steel scent of a hard freeze. I bundled in a stout wool coat that almost swept the ground, pulled on boots and set out westward with Lord Houghton's letter in my pocket.

I took the train as far as it traveled toward Cornwall. I hadn't boarded one since my separation from Cecilia. It was too painful, as if the machine itself wished me harm and would take me to some awful place. But the weather and circumstances, now that an interview had been set, necessitated that I move with speed. It was as though the Messieurs were putting me to a test to see how badly I wanted to speak to them and therefore how soon I would arrive if given a strict deadline and a gathering storm. Whatever ice had lain across the tracks was broken. Hail almost as large as a child's fist replaced sleet and snow, yet somehow the pings and blows didn't break the windows. Steam hissed, the gigantic breathing of the beast that held me captive. At the end of the line, I hired a coach to take me from Bristol down through Exeter. On the approach to the headlands leading to the river, the famous rolling hills, green in summer, consisted of nothing but stubble and frost. I would hear no haunting cry of the curlew echoing on an incoming tide; see no wading birds in the mudflats, just stark saltmarsh. The ancient oak woodland stood devoid of leaves, the farms apart each from the other and no humans in sight, nor any windows close enough for me to detect warmth inside.

Most conspicuously lay large blocks of granite, as well as the cliffs of which the city had been hewn, and as I crossed on the ferry, a bridge to the side was made of that same stone. I imagined being crushed between those blocks. I found the hotel that had been recommended and the man at the desk handed me a message tersely stating that Tweedy and Bond would be waiting for me at an office at the address given at nine o'clock sharp in the morning. I almost left right away to return to London but calmed myself by ordering a portion of duck and a cup of hot cider, the strongest tastes I could muster to slow the motion of my mind and leave me only with sheer sensation on my burnt palate.

Over and over I revisited the image of Deirdre's head hitting the edge of the table, how her body sprawled on the floor, whether she might in fact have been saved. I could recall the exact pitch of Cecilia's opium screams, hear Priscilla's mocking laughter, how she swallowed as the muscles of her legs clenched, the gulping sound as if blood were spurting from her throat. I could smell the sharp tobacco on Bellington's breath and taste the smoke. I wondered whether I could swim across the half frozen Tamar River, first stripping naked so I wouldn't be dragged down as in my dream of the Thames, and whether the bracing water would put an end to me from sheer exposure, or whether my father's crude baptism in the mountain lake had left me encased in an invisible magic sheath. In this fervid swarm I lay down on a mattress half-exhausted by others' restlessness, and sank, not into garbage but into some substance much like it, a gelatin affording the impossible task of trying to drown but not being able, instead breathing in the sear of water, oddly reminiscent of its opposite, fire. I jerked awake, thinking the hotel was in flames, but it was only me, Kilcairn, the man Cecilia once sang of as a small blue spirit inside a yellow flame.

Part III

The Messieurs had their girl serve me tea, though they didn't drink any. The last thing I needed at that moment was any sort of stimulant, but it seemed important to them to watch me hover over a cup of Ceylon, which might lead to soothsaying. Their office overlooked the very spot where the train was planned to cross, as though they had to keep an eye on it. Bond sized me up, one cocked eye trembling, while Tweedy began the sell. "Your advocacy would be strictly on a commission basis. That's the risk you take. If you pull it off, you stand to gain twenty thousand pounds as a fee. It's win or lose, nothing in between."

"Yet we have confidence in you. In one sense, you're a last resort. We too are taking a gamble. But what you pulled off with Norway was brilliant. It was so simple that everybody wondered after why they hadn't thought of it."

"Besides, dear boy, it would be a delicious pleasure to watch Kip Bellington get bested by his former son-in-law. A succés de scandale. The man has concentrated far too much power and is taking over the legislature."

"The publicity value alone is inestimable. His getting whipped in the press shifts the emphasis and balance of power."

It occurred to me to ask these men for greater compensation, or a fee up front. But I know their ilk better than I wanted to. The idea of bringing me in had been cooked up over pipe tobacco, their heads a little light. They were used to making and losing large sums of money, and I represented to them, in some measure, little more than a wager on the running of a gelding. I'd won a big race and gotten beaten badly in the next. Now what?

The next day, I took a detour before returning home, to the cliffs above Strangles Beach, along the treacherous coastline where so many ships ran aground against the rocks. The winter storm had abated, and I watched waves beat the white cliffs until I could no longer feel my cold face.

PART IV
LOIS

IN A REASONABLY SHORT TIME, BACK IN LONDON, I WORKED THE case out, using the existing prospectus and the extant reports of Burnel and other engineers. I asked for the help of a former classmate who was now an esteemed economist and a skilled market bettor. We constructed a compelling comparative analysis, the cheapest way of building the railroad, as well as emphasizing the fact that the piston system of locomotion probably wouldn't work. Finally, we showed the political benefits to as many of the parties involved as possible. Nothing in the proposition stood out as especially new or original. This was more a case of synthesis. I had to produce a brio personal performance in the simplest and most direct terms possible, staked on my reputation as a subtle thinker, making perception into reality, banking in part on the personal drama of having married into the most hated and invulnerable family in England.

I was to return to Cornwall within the week to announce my findings, when I received a note on peach stationery, in a sealed envelope, with no return address. The letter was from Cecilia.

Kilcairn—

Please don't go up against my father. You should never have been forced into our family. Now you are free of us.

The forces against you and me are just too great. You've always felt that everything is in your power. That brutal, overpowering person in you, with its need for cruelty, to receive and inflict pain, will never disappear. For a time, I too wanted to be devoured by you, as a rabbit is by a wolf, but my need for it passed. I don't say my father is any better. I only ask you to step away from what is, in effect, your trial.

I know you are strong, but if you lose, that second public humiliation will obliterate you. I say this all for your sake, not theirs.

Cecilia

If she and I stood up together, it wouldn't matter what else happened. Though I had no assurance that the thoughts in the letter were entirely hers, I recognized the handwriting, still that of a schoolgirl. Without hesitation, I destroyed my report to the railroad, to let them fight it out. I thought their fury would come down upon me, but on the contrary, the parties in dispute came to an understanding after that, with surprising ease, once it became clear that no spectacle of blood sport would take place to keep the MPs amused.

The southern route was agreed on. Bellington's rivals allowed him to purchase stock in the venture. Everybody got something. It turned out that they weren't really enemies after all, just when they wanted to be. I got reminded of just how dispensable my kind was—at best, a court jester who had read Leviathan and knew that the continual and indefatigable generation of knowledge, even if it changes nothing, exceeds the short vehemence of any carnal pleasure. In a month's time I was forgotten again, or if remembered, only as a fly that buzzed near, made a small, insistent noise, and veered off into the afternoon.

When I reached ten years of age, my mother took it upon herself to send me to the Vicar's house to do good works. Despite all the crucifixes that hung in our house, I never saw her pray, at table or elsewhere. When I asked her about it, she replied that it was something you did in private—like a solitary sex act, I suppose she meant—and that it wasn't necessary to say the words aloud or talk about them with someone else. The matter was between you and God.

So it was that I got delivered into the hands of our local Man of the Cloth, though without ever broaching any topic of religion with him, nor him with me. I had imagined that I'd be taken along to visit the sick, or feed the poor, to live out the Beatitudes one by one. But good works, it turned out, meant doing for the Vicar and his wife some of the same chores that I had temporarily been freed from at home. If a barn needed repair, a wall mending, I was just right for the job. As a reward, he let me peruse for an hour, when my tasks were complete, a volume or two in his personal library. He had a marvelous collection of texts by Pliny, Cicero, St. Augustine, and other writers; no novels or poetry were in evidence, nothing of the secular plenitude of Sir Walter Scott, but plenty of classical texts of philosophy and rhetoric crowded the shelves. It must have amused him to watch me thumbing through the pages of books that even he had not opened, reflecting that I couldn't possibly have an idea of what any of them meant.

Most of them enlightened me in the conventional ways, exhorting me to virtue and obedience, civic striving and the betterment of man before God, the Republic, or our peers. Yet I was highly struck by, and committed to memory, a strange passage by Pliny the Elder, the like of which my young eyes had certainly never read. It claimed that:

> Contact with menstrual blood turns new wine sour, crops touched by it become barren, grafts die, seeds in gardens are dried up, the fruit of trees falls off, the edge of steel and the gleam of ivory are dulled, hives of bees die, even bronze and iron are at once seized by rust, and a horrible smell fills the air; to taste it drives dogs mad and infects their bites with an incurable poison.

When alone at home, I strutted around the fields declaiming these words as if I were a great Roman orator. I had no idea what menstrual meant, only that it was an especially terrible kind of blood. I dared not ask my mother or the Vicar either. Some instinct told me that it wasn't the kind of blood drawn on the field of battle.

In general, the visits to the Vicar were uneventful, but another boy spent time there, perhaps for the same reasons as me. That's what I assumed. We spoke little, because we were set to different tasks. Inevitably, we coincided in space. I asked him whether he knew what menstrual meant, and he replied that he wasn't sure, but he thought the word referred to a musician in a traveling show. That made no sense, but I let the matter pass.

Rather, I took to watching him from afar. He was clumsy, given to hitting his thumb with a hammer, tripping over a doorframe, dropping an egg he'd just fetched from under a hen. When the egg broke, he shoved the yolk under some straw and mixed the mess with his foot, hoping that it wouldn't be spotted. All the time he looked nervous. And in fact, one day—perhaps the mistress didn't remember I'd come then, or possibly she didn't care—the Vicar's wife laid into him with a rod, whipping him across the back until he lay trembling against the ground while she berated him for having knocked over a pail of milk. After that incident, I told my mother that I'd rather serve her and father on Saturdays than the Vicar, that I'd prayed on the matter, God had agreed, and that's all I had to say about it. Without much fuss, she discontinued my visits, giving what excuse I know not. Possibly she'd decided that one cannot really get to Heaven on someone else's back after all.

Before long, I prowled the night docks of London in a rain slicker. I had no one in my life, no reason to arrive at my apartment at a certain hour, nothing to entertain me, and no interest in my work. Two women were dead at my hands, and I needed to add a third. Snow and ice had given way to the pasty season of loam, bog, rotten planks with slugs stuck on, yellow foam at the water's edge, silverfish scuttling, ravens scratching themselves between caws. An empty nest, possibly last season's, sat in the crotch of a dwarf pear tree void of fruit.

No one happened by as I wandered from slip to slip, taking in the massive sides of ships, glossy with black industrial paint, or scarred with rust. I'd have to venture into one of the dockside bars. The thought was distasteful. I'd necessarily pick from the usual assortment of working girls, with conventional thoughts and dull dreams, sitting in groups, hats purposely askew to draw the eye, dresses uniformly tight enough to get a man's attention, loose enough to be removed without too much trouble, all of them having the exact same conversation, the one they had yesterday and the one they'd have tomorrow until the time came to speak of wedding vows, unending bliss, children, diaper rash, dog breath, and the faults of one's neighbors. There were no new words to utter in the universe, only gin fizz and other syrupy concoctions laced with alcohol to be sipped slowly, so that the coins in the clutch purse wouldn't deplete before a willing lad approached and offered to take over the bar tab.

But in I went, to a place I'd never entered, thick planks and soiled light, a tavern crackling with the vapors of grease on fresh cod, skillful wenches crisscrossing the floor with pints in either hand. To my relief, the customers were mostly men. If I stayed put, the need for human blood might just pass. I found a bench in the corner, ordered the same as everyone else, and removed a pocket-sized book of Donne's poetry I'd been carrying around with me, reading over and over a single poem, like a pathetic schoolboy. I looked down at the words on the blistered page again, though I knew them by heart.

Oh do not die, for I shall hate
All women so, when thou art gone
That thee I shall not celebrate
When I remember, thou wast one

Each word spoke plain. I imagined Donne dashed off that stanza, putting down the first words that came into his heart. His grief was so great he didn't have time to fool around with art. He only knew what he wanted to say.

A big shaggy fellow occupying the rest of the bench leaned over, gave me the cold eye and said "This in't a library."

I thought of giving him a fresh answer, sure to lead to mutual blows, or just sticking a knife into his gut and quietly leaving. Instead, I answered, "I'm only going over accounts in my ledger."

He squinted down, possibly wondering why there were letters rather than numbers, but decided to forget about the matter, and turned back to his friends, who were going on about lake trout. That's when I spied a woman, about my age, alone, also holding a book in her hand.

I made my way over and held up my own book as a greeting. "May I sit down?"

She looked skeptical, but after a pause, she gestured with her head for me to take a seat. "What's yours?"

"John Keats."

"Sorry don't know him. I'm lost in one of Bridgewater's treatises."

"Who?"

"Frances Bridgewater. It's about the power, wisdom and goodness of God."

"And what does Mr. Bridgewater have to say about it?"

"That a sense of injury implies its opposite—a sense of justice. That all who are capable of anger must also have, to a degree, a capacity for moral feeling."

"So annoyance and hurt lead us to God."

"If we let them."

"You come here alone and don't get bothered?"

"I'm just the eccentric book lady."

"I shouldn't have disturbed you."

"Nonsense. You're the eccentric book man, so we must sit together awhile."

Sandy hair cascaded down her back to her waist. She wore a simple dress, made of homespun cloth, and no makeup. She struck me as a woman who might found a utopian commune. "What do you think of Brook Farm?"

"That ended last year. Didn't you hear? Too many squabbles about money."

"That's sad," I said.

"Don't think I wouldn't have run off and joined it at seventeen. Are you married?"

"I—wasn't expecting such a personal question all of a sudden."

"That was forward of me," she said.

"It didn't work out. Are you married?"

"I still am, legally. But he liked someone else better. They moved to Manchester. I don't know why men are incapable of remaining faithful; none of them, from what I've seen. I'm quite sure you lay with some other woman while you were married." This unexpected verbal slap stung the more because it was true. “That was horrible of me to say.”

“That was the hurt that leads to moral consciousness, right?” I laughed to put her at her ease.

“Nice of you, to ignore my bitter outburst. I’m sure you’re one of the few who stayed true to his woman, and I don’t doubt that the breakup was her fault.”

Now she had me piqued again. What business of hers was it whether I stayed faithful or not, or why we parted? Who would she be to judge in any case? In a single sentence, right after apologizing, she’d managed to insult both Cecilia and me.

“I think I’d better go. I was in the midst of a short walk, and only came in to eat.”

“You’re angry,” she cried. “And it’s my fault. I won’t let you run away upset. Please let me accompany you. I’ve been sitting here far too long. We’ll pretend we’re wandering Brook Farm.”

I didn’t want her company, but to show her that I was able to turn a sense of injury into a sense of justice, as God and Bridgewater had ordained, I had her come along. We made our way along the Regent’s Canal, fronted with small wooden barges that during the day got loaded with timber, burlap bags, barrels of nails, pitch or wine and guided by dockhands with long poles in their hands. Now the barges sat empty and moored, subtly moving, and the only lighted boat to be seen was a floating gin palace on the far shore. The other pedestrians fell away until they left just us walking among factory buildings, the dissipating stench of hot glue, tar, sulfur, and occasional stands of trees that broke up the otherwise unrelieved succession of bricks now blackened, lumber now porous, or lime and fly ash mixed into cement. A zinc sky had been set down over all of it.

“It’s beautiful out tonight,” she said.

There is no question that this woman had served at shelters for the poor and hospices for the elderly. I didn't doubt she loved parakeets, mice, and cats. All I desired was for her to remain quiet long enough for me to feel, as she did, the beauty of the cosmos descended on us, perhaps just the glimmer of a single star that would vouchsafe her opinion that the prospect right before our eyes was, after all, one of delight.

"Men are—monsters. Well, not you."

"Nor your father, of course."

"You know him?"

"That was a witticism."

"Oh. Naturally."

"Well, he was a bounder." The scent of saltmarsh was trying to push away the factory smells, as we neared a grove of trees.

"Why do you speak to men at all?"

"Weakness, I suppose. Besides, they're in the way, and one can't help noticing them. You are terribly attractive physically. The kind who I swear to ignore, then I end up throwing myself on the nearest tick of straw."

"You needn't do so for my sake."

"So, then you don't think I'm pretty?"

"I hadn't thought about it."

"I hate you!"

"I believe our stroll has ended. I'm sorry if I disturbed you with my monstrosity." I turned to walk away. She rushed after and gripped my forearm.

"Please. I don't know what has gotten into me. I'd like to see you. I mean, spend some time together."

"Unhand me, if you don't mind. I've been insulted enough for one day and I don't want to make a habit of getting abused. I sense you have no other way of speaking. You can't help yourself. I understand being impulsive. Please, it's better for both of us that we part company now. I can feel the blood simmer coming on."

"Blood simmer? What a curious phrase." She was trying to put her arms around me, and as I resisted, she forced herself the harder.

"Madam, if I were you, I would be running right now." I grabbed her by the throat and after a struggle, she pushed me away.

"You brutal man! Look! You've left impressions of your fingers on my neck. I've had a good look at you and don't believe the police won't be paying you a visit."

Behind her right ear, a half-moon fought to push off suffocating clouds. The blade of my knife slid quickly into her side as my hand smothered her mouth. The blood flowed with amazing speed. Her knees buckled and I swung her to the side of the path like a drunken dance partner.

I could have gone to jail, but William Gladstone saved me. It was imprudent to have left with a habitué of a tavern, familiar to those around her. Yet the fact that, as she remarked, the men there had ceased to pay attention to her must have meant that they didn't pay so much attention to me. Descriptions of the visitor to her table varied and contradicted one another. The one that the police latched onto was "a tallish man with a book." That wasn't much to go on. I had burned my topcoat and gloves in a nearby factory incinerator, along with her corpse and clothes, after patiently waiting outside for over an hour for the watchman to go off and relieve himself, using a nearby ditch. I knew the area from my early days at Makepeace-Bellington, and I'd been sent over to that factory once to fuss about a large order of ingots.

Gladstone and I had gone to Oxford and distinguished ourselves in the Debating Society. Neither of us was really a drinker. He associated me with the idea of temperance. He'd endorsed me as a candidate before the crisis fell. I filed for an injunction against the City of London for the state of its sewers and the quality of its water in the poorer districts. The hot dry summer of 1846 had sparked a serious outbreak of water-borne enteric fever in the fall. Then came typhus, influenza dysentery, enteric fever. Several of my clients came begging for funds to bury a child or a parent, and surreptitiously I gave enough to a few for funeral expenses. Those around me could desperately have used those twenty thousand pounds I let go of in a sentimental moment, on account of Cecilia's letter.

How is it not possible to stop oneself when you know perfectly well, in the most right part of your mind, that your actions and impulses will assuredly take you to perdition?

In the midst of these epidemics, Gladstone made a speech, quoting from my brief against the city. One of his other pet causes was reclaiming street prostitutes and bringing them to the church. He met them on the street, sometimes late at night, to temporize, evangelize, and reorganize their lives. He cried out that instead of criticizing him amongst fallen women, the citizens and legislators, Anglicans, Episcopalians and Presbyterians, should worry about the men and women falling all around them, reaped by disease.

No matter that he failed to give me credit for my words. When his political sermon had been well received, he sent for me in person. That great man could attract anyone with his arched dark brows, intense eyes, fixed on one's own, the lank hair that flew when he suddenly turned with an idea, even the way his waist coat fell around the hand thrust in his pocket as he searched for the very piece of paper that would back up his argument—in this case, mine.

"Kilcairn, I must say that I was sorry to watch you walk away from your candidacy. You should have come to me for counsel. I hope you know that I stood by you and would have never turned against you."

"I appreciate that, Lord Gladstone."

"Perhaps it's not too late for a political career. No matter that you're a country boy; I also am one, in a manner of speaking—my countryside is Oxford. Yet I hear that you recently walked away from a possibly large sum of money attached to a railroad merger—not wise. You have to build allies and capital."

"I'm pretty sure I did the right thing in that case."

"Only you can know. The cause we share is public health. I am going to push for legislation, taking elements of what you've written here. Your critique builds on the reports of Drs. Smith and Chadwick, making a call for direct action. I believe that next year we can push successfully for a Public Health Bill."

"I'm glad to provide a bit of service to the Kingdom."

"I'm sure you've heard of my visits to the more humble precincts, sometimes criticized, to rescue prostitutes."

"I've made those visits myself."

Gladstone's gaze bore down on me. "Is that an attempt at mirth?"

"By no means. I literally have walked those same neighborhoods, because some of those women and their families are my clients, and also I was surveying the terrain so that I could make my report."

"I've come to resent mockery of my marriage vows. I will never give any of them the satisfaction of replying to their insinuations in public or in private. I will press on with this campaign. Often, those poor deprived women are the first to die. I'd like it if you and I could make the rounds together once or twice."

The police captain who had confronted me about Deirdre's death called me in belatedly about the killing of the book-lady. I did my best to give him an incredulous stare. "Here we are again," I said.

"For very good reasons, I think. You beat us out before, on technicalities, by throwing us off the track with pseudo-science. The semen ploy was clever."

"Ploy? You mean she didn't have a man's sperm inside her?"

"She did, as you know. You were at the trial. But the test was inconclusive. So it could have been anyone's."

"It could be yours, in other words." The captain cuffed me hard upside the head. There was sure to be a bruise. I tried not to take it amiss. He could always be killed, if it came to that.

"This woman Lois Sutter, the one murdered on the Regents' Canal, was seen with someone much like you."

"Was she murdered? I read that she had simply disappeared. I didn't know they'd found her body."

"Well, they haven't. But we don't give up so easily, Counselor. We went back to the tavern for second interviews."

"After so much time? I'm sure the patrons are always drinking, so I guess you can just show up any night of the week or month of the year."

"The composite portrait emerging is of a fellow who looks much like you. Is there something you want to tell us, before matters get ugly? We have positive identification of you that same night, very close by, from a coal whipper who used to work on the docks when you were employed by Makepeace-Bellington."

"There are so many people milling about in such places that your witness is meaningless, especially at this late date."

"I know it was you. At least one person in this world recognizes you for what you are."

"I'd like to help you once again, but I've just been retained by William Gladstone to do work with the poor. You may remember him as the man missing the forefinger on his left hand; or as a current Minister of Sir Robert Peel's government. Unless you have enough evidence to charge me, I'll be going. I am beginning to feel harassed."

The investigation continued, without me, and Gladstone and I went to meet the fallen women.

Part V

MATTIE

Though I wasn't thinking about it at the time, the initial visit to the slums with Gladstone in my company gave me an alibi to be seen in those places at night, on an errand of God. Even retroactively, I had cover. Unlike Gladstone, I wasn't even married, nor attached to a woman. I was a bachelor errant, protégé of a man who had just helped found The Holy and Undivided Trinity College at Glenalmon, a man whom all of us knew would someday be the Prime Minister of our country. I became one of his speechwriters, not a fact he mentioned to anyone, but he did pay me a sum for my work. If I'd been smart—if I'd just kept myself under control—I would have risen, possibly faster and higher than on my first try. Nothing is so quickening to one's prospects as the patronage of a powerful man—and in this case, despite his quirks and prejudices, one who was truly enlightened. Unlike Bellington, Gladstone was someone I wanted to be and who didn't seem to have a yen to destroy me.

Perhaps that victory would have happened, if I hadn't accepted the gratitude of one of those women after I accompanied her to an evangelical service of the Church Penitentiary Association. Things had been going along well, and I sometimes worshipped to keep him happy, and also on the off chance that God might actually one day show up. Minister Gladstone had never asked me about my own religious beliefs; he just assumed I must share his.

Mattie could best be described a voluptuary. There was nothing fallen about her: not the sheen of her hair, the luster of her skin, the firmness of her breasts and limbs, the gleam of her pupils. She's not the woman you trot out to prove the pathos of the situation. She came across smart and in her own way, driven. She had just slipped between the cracks of several better situations, her stubborn and luxuriant nature the probable cause of those situational failures. She ended up a prostitute, as a Latin teacher might end up serving her former students beef stew in a refectory.

When we arrived, it was clear at once that the women of the CPA hated her. They made her sit in the back, wedged between two hard-used and dire strumpets now turned repentant, two bookends of sin holding up a single gilt tome of Kama Sutra. The ladies in charge tried to force me to leave, so utter strictness could begin, but I stood along the wall with my hands folded, pretending to pray to their Rhubarb Jesus. In the middle of the service, which was really little more than a catalogue of tasks and taboos that could better have just been posted on the dormitory wall, without all the spit and sweat, she gave me a pleading look, and without knowing quite what she had in mind, I assented with a nod. She pretended to need to throw up, producing a couple of convincing retches, and with the disease that had been running round London, the biddies were relieved to see her go. They took no chances.

That left the two of us outdoors. "Where would you like to go?"

"Let's eat, but nothing extravagant," she proposed.

"I'll go into this nice Moroccan restaurant around the corner. I'll order Khobz bread and a stew of potatoes, lentils, and apricots. I'll ask them to wrap it all up."

"To where?"

"I'll rent us a room in which to eat it."

"A dining room?"she asked, her playful eyes shining.

"A hotel room. The Turks in this quarter don't care who we are."

When we stood inside the bedchamber, underlain with an unexpectedly pretty patterned carpet, only a little musty, she said, "There's something I want to give you." She removed her coat and swept her arms down her body, as if to say, "This is all on the menu as well, and it's free."

I have understood since childhood that nothing is free. Yet I chose to overlook that fact. She sat on my lap feeding me dollops of stew on wheat bread. Mattie tasted much like the stew—warm, full of enough spices to prickle the tongue. Even more, she enjoyed me just as much. Not only did she not exist as a "fallen woman," she in no way resembled a whore.

In the late morning of the next day, we awoke after a deep sleep; probably the best night's sleep of my life, and wandered the neighborhood, stopping to listen to a dulcimer, a goatskin drum, and the longest flute I'd ever seen. I told her I had to return to work and open my office. She transferred a kiss from her lips to mine with a sugar-sticky finger and gave me a hooded look, as if she wore a veil. It didn't occur to me until she'd travelled far down the street to offer her money for a cab.

I couldn't find fault, really, with the two of us having spent a night together. But I got summoned that week to Gladstone's office, supposedly to help him with an upcoming speech.

"Look, old man. I'm sure you've done nothing wrong. But you do have a reputation as being a bit eccentric, and well—a past life, about which I wish to know nothing beyond what I know already."

"I thank you for that."

"This woman you accompanied to the Penitentiary Association—when she feigned sickness to leave—she put you in a tough spot. I apologize for using you as an escort, and I promise not to do it again."

"As you wish."

"If she were to come around—women can get notions in their heads—discourage her; straight out turn her away. Some fallen women don't want to be lifted up."

"I'll do as you ask."

Gladstone seemed to accept this and he turned his attentions elsewhere, as if throwing a switch. "So then, about this speech I'm to give. How should we end it?"

I thought no more of Mattie, except as one remembers a polished mineral fragment that slips through a hole in one's trousers pocket, to be lost on the street. I was doing what Gladstone asked—building capital, working the neighborhoods to gather testimony for the Public Health Law prospectus, running my law office, helping his societies with publicity. If you ride on a shark's back, the best thing to do is lie flat so you won't fall off. The shark can move a lot faster than you, and you don't really want it to remember often that you're holding on. Peel had fallen sick; his government had disintegrated in part over import tariffs on corn and grain. Now Gladstone worked as an MP in the opposition, and it hadn't become clear when and how he would surge to his next high post.

We began to have success when the city adopted piecemeal recommendations I had passed on from a Dr. Raintree, who had spent time studying the outbreaks. Pump handles got removed, and we discouraged people from doing business with suppliers who drew water from the Thames downstream, after many sewers had flowed in. We asked citizens to take the simple step of boiling water. We'd made things cleaner all around.

Yet one night, after making an informal neighborhood inspection, I entered the premises of three prostitutes who lived together in quarters fit for squatters. We snacked on chicken that had been left sitting out for God knows how long, and limp potatoes. I can't offer the excuse that I got drunk, as I only watched them circulate a bottle. What happened next best goes by the name of an orgy. Their nimble fingers flew over me until I had been made nothing but skin, and they simply lifted their dresses over their heads, as they wore no undergarments. Their boozy kisses rained over my anatomy, followed by slurping, smacking, licking, groping. I felt slathered with jelly. I rolled each on her back, stomach, side, pummeling, twisting, sliding, holding myself back from finishing so that the grappling match could continue. They cackled and whooped, while taking turns leaping from the bed so that I would chase them and throw them down. My climax came like being struck by lightning but having the misfortune of remaining alive.

The next day, I soaked in a tub until the water turned stone cold. After nearly rubbing myself raw, I reflected on the fact that I stood as the poorest of exemplars of practices leading to the good public health to which I'd devoted so many hours. I'd put myself on the same level as the most ignorant dweller of East London, not having protected myself in any way. What is more, if the news got back to Gladstone, my nascent political career would be over once again. Yet I returned to those women on three separate occasions. Once such a woman opens your trousers, unless you pay her, all pretense of social difference goes away, and you have given her every advantage. I could not even console myself that they were particularly attractive or seductive. How could I have once been attached to the radiant Cecilia and settle for this grit in my craw? But why had I fixated on these three harpies? Unlike those in Macbeth, they had no magic to attract me except the usual banal spell of opening their legs and mouths.

I veered between self-loathing and craving. Perhaps the neighbors knew but held a code of silence so that my interest in their welfare wouldn't ebb. Perhaps they understood their self-interest better than I did mine. Nonetheless, I paced my room asking myself whether it wasn't best to kill all three, lure them to a field for another supposed orgy. But even if I felled one, the others might attack me.

The most I could do for the moment was not go back. My occasional propensity for supernatural thinking manifested in my belief that if I scurried around doing good deeds, or lost myself inside high-minded philosophical writing, I'd ward off demons. I was no better than a Maori kneeling before the earth mother to deliver me from harm.

In the midst of this moil, Mattie showed up on my steps on an evening when I'd just put on a clean shirt to go out and stood reflecting on how silver the sky had become. There was no sense participating in a standoff at the door, one I knew I'd lose, so I invited her in.

"You don't look happy to see me."

For an instant I considered trying to work up some happiness. Her gown of batik made her much more attractive to both eye and mind than my dreary plan to go the club, just to remind the other gentlemen that I still mattered, and to suffer pretense of bonhomie, as if we were all truly brothers just because we'd once worn the same shield emblazoned on a garment.

But it remained better not to give an opening. I held no rancor, but I had to work some up, like spit on the driest of days. "It's brazen for you to come here."

"More brazen than your visits to the neighborhood? More brazen than the first and only night we spent together?"

"It's just that, Mattie. I've been forbidden to see you."

"By your mother?"

"You know damned well by whom."

"Normally I'd be sympathetic, love, but you've been flaunting your cock like the feathered ones with crowns that men let spar in the churchyard."

"I've broken myself of those bad habits."

"I'm not so sure." She straddled my lap. I caught hold of her wrists before her hands could go anywhere. "I know your sort, Kilcairn. Noble one second, a prize pig the next."

"What do you want?"

"So it's like that? All right then, let's talk business. I want money. You didn't pay me the first time around."

"Is that all, Mattie? Let me go for my wallet."

"I don't think you understand. You're not paying for my cunt. I already gave you that, on the house. And sad to say, I fancied you such that I was willing to keep giving it. But I vowed to be a good girl for your sake. I made you help me get kicked out of the Bible brothel, and I felt bad about it. We whores have a lot of faults, but we do know our station in life. And then I come to find out that you've been dipping your quill in three murky inkwells.

"As I said, it was a mistake."

"A huge one. So this is how it goes. You're going to pay me an allowance of 100 quid a month for as long as I say so."

"I don't have that kind of money."

"You should have thought of that before you turned down the railroad fellows. Everybody, even we ignorant street girls, knows that you kicked over a pot of gold."

"There was no guarantee I'd win. The offer was all or nothing."

"All of a sudden he doubts his prowess. Besides, you have a law practice and it also came to my attention that you were handing out free pounds sterling to the downtrodden just because their fathers died. So let's hear no more of your trouble with finances. I want a hundred quid right now."

I fetched my wallet. "This is it. One time only."

"You eat tripe when you could have a nice skirt steak. I stand far above those hideous she-toads. You hurt my feelings. Do you understand? I spent my own pence to come see you. All I wanted was to give, not to take. How many people like that do you have—real friends? Forget about the sex—I just liked you, remembering how we laughed running down the street and listened to the dulcimer. I sat in your lap and fed you from my hand. You're staying away from me because you want to remain safe. But you can't get away from yourself. Do you think that industrialist brought you down—or his wife—or his daughter? You knew exactly what you were doing. I have no pity for your mistakes.

"And lots of Londoners laugh at you, not only the high-born ones. The humble folk you're serving—the horrid sluts, the runts shitting themselves. They believe they're better off than you. You should be better than them. They should resent you a little because they want to slip into your skin and exist as you do.

"I did pity you when we met. There I sat, without a penny, a woman who let herself be slapped around by men who go in and out of jail. You touched my heart. But you smashed it with your heel. Yes, I can use the money. But I savor the thought of you paying me a hundred quid a month, so that once every fortnight you'll think of me, as if it were our anniversary."

She kissed me on the mouth with watery eyes and took her leave.

When Mattie next showed her face, a month to the day from when I'd last seen her, I was working at my office. It's a good thing I hadn't kept a secretary. She apologized, but thought it was better than going to my house, which I had forbidden. Not knowing what else to do, I counted one hundred quid in petty cash out of the drawer, and told her next time I would simply leave it in the bottom of an urn, promptly at 8 a.m. on the day agreed upon. If the money was gone at 8:30 of the clock, she was not to protest that it couldn't be found.

She leaned over—exposing what was not covered by a brocaded dress she'd doubtless bought with the previous payment, and tried to clasp my hand. "It's not the money I want. It's you." I gave no answer. Mattie jumped up, grabbed hold of her quetzal-plumed hat, and stormed out. Though I had met her terms, she sent a note to me a few days later that she had plans to speak to Willy about the Three Graces. No doubt she'd get into his office by putting on a show of repentance. I would be portrayed as the lowest point of her "fall," and she would weep for him to lift her up on his strong shoulders once again. Mattie waxed eloquent, a creature of apparent reason with a great gift of rhetoric. Had she put her mind to it, she could have rivaled John Charles Ryle in the pulpit. If she'd just remained a blackmailer, I might have let her predatory behavior go on for a few months.

I decided to take a few days off work. Writing with my opposite hand, I sent a letter through the post, anonymous, asking her to come round at eight in the evening on a Thursday. When she showed up, I gestured her inside, where I'd set out licorice tea with buttery almond crumpets. I did my best not to lay on too thick my speech about her having been right. I didn't announce a romantic vacation for the two of us. I simply mused that I needed to get out of town, and would she like to come along with me to Margate for the weekend? I wanted to leave for the station in an hour. I did not wish for her to have the chance to boast about the fact that she was about to embark on a seaside vacation with a known man of quality.

She insisted she would need to pack.

"No, let me buy you a few nice things there, a bathing costume and a couple of summer dresses. I promise that my taste for fashion will be up to the occasion."

"You do dress well. I trust you to make the right choices. But it's impulsive to leave like this, with no warning."

"Any more impulsive than our first and only night together?"

Her answer was arms thrown around me.

Mattie and I arrived in Margate without raising any particular or immediate interest in our persons. I was not listed in a guide someone had left in our night table, "Waterplaces of Great Britain and Fashionable Directory." I would recommend it to anyone as an amusing thumb-through, worthy of a penny novel. We were nobody—two more tourists of the many thronging the town. We stayed at the Cinque Port Arms, despite not having made reservations beforehand. Truly it was an occasion to get lost in a crowd. I avoided falling into the trap of chatting up other couples who might want to become vacation friends.

The Baths, Billiard Rooms, Booksellers, and Brewers lay at our disposal. The Dressmakers, Wine Merchants, Perfumers stood at the ready. And had we wished, the Ironmongers, Cheese-mongers, Fishmongers, Bonnet Makers, Chandlers, Glaziers, and even the redoubtable Joseph Hollams, who by himself practiced the professions of Tailor, Draper, Tea Dealer and Undertaker, at 137 High Street, would have made time in their busy schedules for us. Tourists are the lifeblood of the town, and merchants are their servants.

We were content on the first morning after our arrival to lounge on our terrace, watching the steam packets come and go from the pier head. Later we relaxed at the Albion vapor baths. Even Hazardous Row was lovely for a walk alongside the water. Then, as I promised, I accompanied Mattie to the dressmaker, who luckily had the right size bathing costume in stock, and who promised to tailor a gown fit for any fine occasion, dining, theater or dance, having it ready for the very next day. It was a gown Mattie would probably never wear. She had agreed with me to supply false names at the desk, those of a married couple, William and Mary Brooke, of which there are many in the world. I simply asked her to give me time to get used to our new arrangement.

Sailboats smoothly cut through the waves under vast white clouds. Laborers provided a remarkable spectacle as they drove horse-drawn coaches straight down in the water, up to their haunches in surf, to load the frigate Buenos Ayres where it stood offshore. From every upper window a wayfarer seemed to wave at those promenading below them on High Street. The hexagon of the lighthouse and St. John's stone church competed with elderberry trees, thatched mangers, and arches of the Dan de Lion for most picturesque prospect.

The problem, despite all her hard words against me, and desperate threats, lay in that Mattie still drew me. So pick up the cream dress we did, and in the marketplace snagged an invitation to a dance to be held at a ballroom where half the registry glided while the other half rested from the day's labors.

The next day we wandered to the chalk cliffs, where we found a cave. Inside it we kissed like children. Into this dream I fell, as one of the comets studied by Isaac Newton to understand gravity, in the autumn sky streaks into nothingness, never hitting the earth.

All bode well, until we made the mistake of visiting a pub, where I watched Mattie put away pint after pint, until she became abusive again, first under her breath, then louder. I might have suffered this outburst, had it been tempered with her usual eloquence, but she let fly a string of loud profanity, asking how a boot-licker and a cock-chafer ended up together; talking of pricks, pussies, quims and piss, snatch, Sodom, strumpet, tarnal rigs and twats, and ended up calling me a whoremonger, to the astonishment of the gathered patrons. I guided her outdoors with a smile, apologizing and mentioning that her mother had just died and that she was mad with excessive grief, so I'd have to send her back to Putney on the first morning packet. On the way out, she began to speak of Gladstone again, in threatening tones, and demanded that we find a justice of the peace and get married at once, rousing him from his bed if necessary.

When she had calmed to a state of mere boozy umbrage, followed by creeping melancholy, I told her that a walk to the cliff cave under the waning moon would cure our ills. At an overlook, I recited a tale my father once related in an expansive moment, about a man who sang in the church of Zennor, and the mermaid who lured him away. We picked our way over sand and rocks, until at length we sat in the cave, her resting between my legs, with her back up against my breast. And that is when, removing a length of piano wire I'd brought along, in my first intention, before she seduced me again with her blithe and mercurial spirit, I strangled her. I wrapped the wire around her throat, pulled it tight, and when she could no longer breathe and lay among the tidal pools where minnows come and go, I dragged Mattie down to the edge of the white cliffs and threw her into the outgoing current of the sea.

The weekend in Margate had whetted my appetite, rather than giving me closure. I returned to Mattie's neighborhood on the slightest pretext, defying logic and the law, and easily found a girl willing to accompany me to a lover's lane lined with oaks to share kisses, then to wait while I procured us cheese sandwiches wrapped in butcher paper, and a half-magnum of champagne. I persuaded her that a walk through an abandoned kiln would be romantic, and inside, let her speak of her love of spun sugar and rainbows, ponies and paperweights, laughter and roses and sunsets, Jesus and Mary and Saint Cecilia, her birthday patroness, and then I killed her with one quick slash to the throat.

Her tedious view of life may have brought on the mortal blow, or maybe I was just going to do it no matter what. But her unfortunate mention of the name Cecilia, while a sheer coincidence, surely sealed her fate. How far I had fallen. As I stood over her still warm corpse, it occurred to me that I had returned depressingly to the beginning of my career as a murderer. This sad escapade in some way stood as an impoverished version of what I had done to the flower girl, sans ambience, rhythm, motion, or motivation. The deceased gave me no pleasure. I had felt no sense of attraction, no sexual surge, no thrill, no blood rage. I'd have been better off knocking her senseless with a brick and leaving her alive. As in my passionate interludes with Priscilla, I had never wanted to think of this activity as art, never wanted to become self-conscious, as though "technique" were the important part. Yes, I did harbor some pride at the immediacy of the deaths I caused, whether by slicing or strangling, the knowledge that the victim died almost instantaneously.

Yet this particular murder simply made me feel bored. It might have sufficed, by sending me into a period of quiescence. I strung up the rainbow girl by her legs, leaving the corpse hanging by a rafter in a far corner of the kiln. This involved climbing, gymnastics, an element of risk in that I might fall, welcome in that it held off the tedium and lent at least a fleeting sense of accomplishment to the day. Somebody would find her, not soon, and when they did, she would already have rotted substantially. As ever, they'd ascribe it to the Gentleman Killer, though I'm not really sure they believed in him anymore. There was speculation—I heard through legal circles—that they had wrongly made a single suspect, a composite, out of two or three different men doing similar crimes.

As if in defiance, and to prove to myself that I could do whatever I want, I found in turn a schoolteacher, a dance instructor, and a missionary traveling through London. I had sex with two of them, without appetite, only to more easily get them alone. The missionary I spared out of some absurd sense that it would be wrong to defile her body in any way, and that it might keep her from the Heaven in which she believed, and I did not. There, at least, was a pang of conscience to show that I could still feel something.

The one unexpected, however, was a woman of independent means, about to embark on a prolonged trip to America, and out looking for another hat, as she felt she was not yet elegant enough for an Atlantic crossing. She was brimming with a sense of adventure and incautiously, I invited her to my flat for a sensual sendoff. I had argued in vain to myself that it was in both our best interests to remain with her on the posh avenue on which we found ourselves, mingling among passersby as a church clock struck for vespers. Once we were abed, I covered her with tender kisses and began to relax, feeling an unbidden peace descend on me, enough so that I took up a strange notion that I might ask her to postpone her trip. Her unfortunate answer sealed her demise. "I would, but my plans are firm. The world awaits my arrival. I only bedded you to begin my adventure. I recognized you at once as Bellington's man, the one who lost a fortune in the railroad and was abandoned by his wife. I saw you that night at the ball. Some of the women were laughing at you, but I felt pity."

Out came the scarf, and she'd had her last adventure.

Making a cold analysis of my life, which struck me more than anything as a prolonged study in failure, I began to entertain the thought of killing myself. It seemed that I would never stop murdering, no matter what. I spent an entire day lying in bed, missing several appointments at the office. Apathy descended upon me. Steak tasted of paper, wine of vinegar, and cake of sand. Weeks passed without my making an appearance at the club. I lost weight and didn't notice for a time that my suits were growing shabby, as I had not bothered to have them cleaned. I dismissed the cleaning lady over nothing, and my apartment began to accumulate dust and unwashed dishes. I lost a simple legal case over back taxes, probably merely because I looked so haggard and had to endure the justified, withering scorn of my client. I was suspicious that people had begun to talk of me, as I suffered their rare stares, keeping my head down as I hurried by, holding down my hat against a gust of wind.

I was strangely heartened to be able to feel disgust for myself, to feel sick about what I had done; to know without equivocation that it was wrong, depraved. This knowledge had come over me many other times, and I swore to change. But that oath would be carried out with the next day's tide. This time, I had to bring myself back to whatever passed for normalcy in England. I went to the lodging of my former housekeeper, begged her to come back, sent my suits out, got my hair cut, and began to eat properly again. I still had no appetite to see men from Oxford and Cambridge, but I resolved to spend the night out, alone, but in a place of public entertainment.

When I was studying at Oxford, I made the acquaintance of Isabelle, an émigré I hired as a French tutor, as I wanted to be able to read the great works in the original. She was a lover of literature, most especially the comedians and satirists, Molière and Rabelais. Inevitably, when we went out for a drink—wine, of course—she would end the evening with the words "Bring down the curtain, the farce is played out." A playful smile graced her petite face at that moment, as we lingered at the stoop. I never could tell whether she wanted me to kiss her, and though I'd been with a couple of women, in her case, I couldn't work up the courage. I had it in my mind that it was important to be a gentleman with her. I found myself half in love as we lingered over the subtleties of verb declensions and how a single word, as she often said, might alter the meaning of an entire paragraph, page, chapter, or even book.

We had a habit of watching the swans in the early evening, gliding across the pond, oblivious to our eyes on them. The sheen on the lake made me think on Isabelle's skin, and I would then turn to watch her brown eyes watching the swans. I wanted to tell her that I cared for her, for the incongruity between Gargantua and Pantagruel and her delicate frame, which moved with an unforced grace. We bought one sandwich to share; that was our habit. My mates thought I was dating her and were shocked to find out that this was not the case. I was told that every young man on campus wanted her. They paid her for tutoring French even when they hadn't the slightest interest, just to be around her, in the hope they might attract her admiration, thence her desire. But as far as anyone could tell, she only had eyes for me. Act now, my friend Rex advised, not gently. You don't leave a ravishing creature like her just lying around. You lie around with her, with your clothes off.

I knew this to be the case, but I couldn't make myself initiate an overture. I imagined that both of us had taken some unspoken oath of purity. Until I made up my mind that she was a woman, after all, and that a man and a woman in close proximity must go one way or another, because platonic friendship between them simply cannot last. A woman always wants more, insisted Rex.

I made up my mind to broach the subject with Isabelle on Saturday, but as we took yet another walk in the park, me grabbing a handful of petals from a flowering bush, crushing them in my hand and wanting to spread the perfume on her neck, I decided that Tuesday would be the day—then Thursday, then the following Saturday. One morning as I sat on the steps of the library on campus, I saw Rex and Isabelle walk across the campus, hand in hand. He stooped to kiss her, and her lovely face and nubile body yielded with a slight tremor, as I had always imagined she would, had I done the same.

Right away I knew what a fool I'd been. Isabelle had given me every chance. My unaccustomed timidity had done me in, as had my need to watch her float before me inside a golden bubble, more of an idea than a person. The most I could say is that when we embraced to say goodbye, I'd gotten close enough to know the scent of her skin, the skin that Rex no doubt covered with kisses in private. I never spoke with Rex again, not so much out of anger as out of embarrassment. I sent a note to Isabelle letting her know I would no longer be taking French lessons. She wrote back "Bring down the curtain, the farce is played out."

I knew she didn't mean the words unkindly. They were a way of letting me down, as well as an epitaph, tinged with regret, for our short season together. In the months afterward, I bedded every girl I could find, nearly ruining my marks for that semester. I thought of dropping out of school, just so our paths wouldn't cross, but she was discreet and managed to continue tutoring and seeing Rex out of my sight, until she flitted off elsewhere, leaving Rex, too, with a broken heart.

PART VI
VALERIE

THE NIGHT I MET VALERIE WAS THE LEAST PROMISING FOR ROMANCE. I had just come close to killing yet another woman, one I met in Vauxhall Gardens. I went to watch the ropewalkers do their act. As the ladies sheathed in the lightest of cloth traverse that stretch of hemp, not looking down at their petite feet, they seem about to fall, but seldom do. I struck up a conversation with one of the rope walkers after, as she turned prettily in the footlights so that the spangles on her skirt glittered.

She agreed to take the boat over into London with me. A man dressed in a fine vest and suit, black as an undertaker's, approached me and gave my hand three friendly pumps.

"Kilcairn!" As he spoke, asking me why I hadn't been to the club in so long, I listened, hoping he'd mention his name. For an instant, I wanted to put my arms around him and press him close, like a brother. Yet that impulse was swiftly followed by something like nausea. I made excuses, promised to visit soon. His eyes shifted to my erstwhile companion. If he suspected an assignation, he gave no sign of it. I took my leave and the girl, discreetly, waited until my "friend" was out of sight before following me out of Vauxhall and down to the pier to climb aboard the boat. On board, she guided me to an unlit corner and pressed her minute body, no more than four stone in weight, against my side.

She made it clear that she couldn't wait to get to a hotel, apartment, or whatever place I might be headed. She didn't ask whither, only clung to me as I might cling to a plank in the Irish Sea, wondering which way the waves were going to push me, toward victory or drowning.

We disembarked, a black slosh of waves beneath kissing the dirty shore. As we walked, she spoke of how she'd made a vow not to get into another relationship with a man, but she could feel there was something special about me.

The surface of the river looked greasy, as if the barges had all left their scum behind before plowing on. As I crossed Blackfriar's Bridge with her, I felt it wasn't safe to throw her body in. The nameless gentleman had seen us. I made an excuse and parted, leaving her holding a stick of licorice she'd never gotten around to eating.

A few days before, overcome by a sudden sense of terror, barely able to breathe, I had the idiotic idea of accosting a woman in the dark in a fairly public place, near a band shell. She was wearing a fur stole much like one that Priscilla used to use. I didn't see her face; rather I approached her from behind and threw her to the ground. As we wrestled in silence and I tried to get to my knife, strangely, she didn't scream. She was unbelievably strong for a woman dressed so well. I wanted to get my hands on her throat, just in case she should decide to cry out, but she pressed her hand against my face, her nail catching the corner of my eye, rose up, hit me with a rock hard upside the head, making me see stars and pushed me off her, so that I lay on my back on the ground. The lady ran off around the corner and into the light, where I could hear the voices of other people, so I fled into a nearby street, into a tavern, surrounded by its smoke, talk and laughter and the smell of old beer. I couldn't know whether she had gotten a glimpse of my face.

In the bathroom, I found a cleaning rag, and wiped the blood from my hair, soaping and rinsing it. When the blood had clotted, I pushed my way again through the human forest of animated mirth, and stepped back outside.

As I toddled down the empty street, letting vapors trail off of me into the night, a step behind startled me. I whirled. A lady in a smart red pea coat and gloves, smiled out of one side of her face. She was sloe-eyed yet had an appearance of alacrity even greater than my obvious wariness.

"Heavens. Did I startle you?"

"No, not at all. I just didn't hear anyone behind me until you came so close."

"Are you always listening for someone behind you?"

"Yes. I'm afraid so."

"Perhaps you should keep better company. Did you think someone was sneaking up to murder you?"

"Possibly."

"You didn't hear a cab pass a moment ago? No loud hooves clopping like the moons of doomsday crashing down?"

"No. I was thinking about something else."

"Well it had me as a passenger, on my way back from the opera."

"I haven't attended in some time. What show did you see?"

"Verdi's Ernani."

"Three men in love with the same woman. All they do is destroy one another, while she prospers. Ernani poisons Elvira and himself, and there's an end of it. The show has cracks, but some of the arias are worth three encores with the right voice behind them."

"I'm impressed. My companion knew nothing of Verdi and said the whole score would sound better if played on accordion."

"Doesn't everything?"

"Do you know the Mackenzies?"

"I'm afraid not. I'm shy by nature and don't get out as much as I should. Tonight is an exception."

"You can't be shy and stand talking to a woman in the middle of the night. Where have you been visiting?"

"Traipsing through the sewers of dear London."

"Don't disparage our beautiful city. She's a lady of a certain age, yet still has the power to attract."

"In truth, I sat in attendance at Vauxhall, I'm ashamed to say."

"Don't be ashamed. At least you can eat peanuts while you watch the show. You can't do that at Covent Garden. If I'd have known, I would have skipped out on Rudy and accompanied you."

"Certainly, I would have liked that. I'll invite you some time. Why did you dismount from that cab in the middle of an empty street?"

"On a whim. Slumming, I guess. Why, are you dangerous?"

"I might be."

"We shall see."

She reached out and brushed my cheek. "Your eye is weeping. Have I touched you so greatly in so short a time?"

"I scratched myself with a quill. I can be clumsy."

"Writing your memoirs?"

"It's much too soon for that. I'm not quite done living."

"When next we meet, I shall supply you with a balm sure to heal you. We can't go around this world all banged up. How about tomorrow for a lunch of pheasant at my favorite restaurant?"

"And the earth was without form, and void; and darkness was upon the face of the deep. And the Spirit of God moved upon the face of the waters." That was my favorite Bible passage as a child. I would move my lips and recite those words when night terrors overcame me, bathing my sheets in sweat. The passage was scary and comforting at the same time. I had the image of a literal face skimming over the waters, looking down into them for something beneath, some answer to a question that hadn't even been formed yet. I liked it that both verses began with the word "and," a word about which I'd never thought. Even though the idea expressed was about beginning, it seemed there was no beginning, and no end, no birth or death either. When I had dreams of drowning, so far below the water that no light broke through the surface, and woke stifling a cry, I reminded myself that God watched the face of the waters and searched into the face of the deep, and there he would find me and lift me with his hand into the air. I never dared utter those thoughts to anyone. I just existed in the void, in an earth without form.

Valerie persuaded me to have dinner with her high-flown friends and we all attended John Gay's The Beggar's Opera. They had a box seat, with blue velvet cushions, and our host joked that we would be easy targets for an assassination. Better the assassin would use a knife, he said, like the Gentleman Killer. The host had no direct experience of war, it seemed, but his son had served alongside Lieutenant Pottinger, who disguised as a holy man travelled via Peshawar to Herat, to help the Shah of Persia's army besiege the city. While the father joked about death, the son stared through his opera glasses without comment at the unfolding spectacle of Lucy trying to poison Polly onstage.

I wanted to be the one who passed unremarked. Whenever I was with Valerie, her shock of red hair an exuberant beacon, I felt that someone hovered close by us, waiting to hurt us. All I wanted was peace, to leave behind the horror. We ate scones by a primrose bush while a robin provided us with a theme song for our newfound affection.

Her lips felt like a gust of moist soul as harmless and pleasant as a summer mist when the clouds gather and part, affording peeks at the sun. She had a favorite song, which she would sing to me while she combed her permanent tangle of hair and plucked the dead strands from the bristles of the brush.

By all we both remember of the past,
When thy young beating heart with mine first met
By that warm kiss, the dearest and the last,
Whose sweetness on my lips is lingering yet
By thy free vow to dare with me the blast,
Nor in the world's frown suffer one regret
By all the love thou gav'st me & still hast,
My heart defies thine ever to forget.

Part VI

Unlike Cecilia, Valerie didn't know how to play a piano, but her warm yet quiet soprano, with a hint of tremolo, needed no accompaniment. I didn't want to be so fond of her, didn't want to flirt with the word love ever again, but I couldn't help myself.

Things went along well until one night, in her company, as we promenaded downtown, a young fellow in a broad straw hat that slipped over his brow followed at a close distance as we made our way along a street festival, ears filled with the half-tone of Chinese strings and nostrils almost clotted with the smell of inferior meat dripping fat from a brazier onto coals. I asked Valerie to pick up the pace and then slow down, the youth mimicking our speed all the while. We turned into a blind alley and when he also entered, I whirled, got him into a quick headlock and threatened to break his neck. The alarm on Valerie's face quickly made me regret my decision, but there was nothing to do but press on. "What do you want from me? Speak up."

He whimpered like a dog that has lost hope of finding its master. "They say you know where my sister is."

"I'm sure I never met her."

"My cousin claims you went to a party with my sister three months ago and no one has seen her since. She might have gone to Scotland, only we checked with our family in Aberdeen and she hasn't turned up." Valerie was listening all the while, and her expression was not disapproving, just curious.

"And you are only confronting me now?"

"You'll beg my pardon, sir, but it took me this long to locate you. A waiter gave us a detailed description and that's all we had to go on. We went to the police, but they didn't want to get involved. Apparently, you beat them at their own game, and they don't want to waste their time on a rumor."

"I don't blame them. As for the description, I look like everybody, just another poor sod in a top hat. What was her name?"

"Tess. She speaks with a stutter." The first woman I beat senseless did stutter, yet that could have just been from the sheer panic of seeing me with a blade in my hand.

"Excuse me for saying so, but do I look like the sort of man who would consort with your sister?"

"No sir. But I had to be certain. I'm sure you understand."

"You have the wrong man. If I ever see you near me again, I'll thrash you unto darkest death. Now get out of here."

When he had left, Valerie smiled. "You scared him with that threat."

"It's only a figure of speech. I wish the poor fellow no harm."

"Don't you think all of us are capable of taking the life of a person?"

"No. Do you?"

"Of course. Hobbes says without the social contract, we'd live by force, eliminating those who don't suit us. That's why we need a sovereign."

"This is a philosophical discussion, then."

"At the moment."

"So, you're not planning to snuff me out?"

"Not yet." She laughed with a girlish peal. I was touched by her feminine attempt to fancy herself as a bleak assassin. That fantasy didn't go at all with the elaborate lavender stitching on her blouse, which I squinted at and tried to decipher, as if there were a message in it meant for me.

Part VI

I met Valerie's parents: Tom, a bureaucrat and sportsman, and Tina, a one-time evangelist and swimming champion. I liked them at once. They took us to the hippodrome, and she won on almost every horse, eating beef stew between races to keep up her energy, as if she herself were going to ride the next mount.

Unlike Priscilla, Valerie didn't boast a tiny waist; rather, she was formed in the athletic, robust mold of her parents—sturdy. When I brought Valerie to my law office and explained to her that I was an advocate for the poor, sometimes working pro bono, other times for meager sums, she seemed surprised.

"Is it really that out of character?"

"I would expect you in starched apparel at Heidelberg, giving lectures on philosophy in fluent German."

Valerie asked for the first time to visit my flat. She wore an aqua dress trimmed in lace, accentuating her cobalt eyes. She wandered around, picking up an oar I still had from my rowing days at Oxford.

"You could kill a man with this."

"That has never occurred to me in all the years I've owned it. You have a macabre mindset."

"Do I? More so than yours?" And with that she began to undress, as if it were the most natural thing in the world, as if, in fact, I weren't there at all. Her almost swarthy skin, with a light coat of fine hair on her arms, put me in mind of a clay figure to be worshipped.

Dress and girdle tossed somewhat carelessly on a chair, her thick brown nipples erect, the dark bush between her legs full and untrimmed, she stood before me, posture perfect but legs spread somewhat apart, as if daring me to penetrate her.

"I want to lie with an experienced man. And I'm sure you've been with more than a few women."

"Seven or eight," I lied.

"How many of them were prostitutes?"

"One or two, I guess."

"I'm quite sure you've lain with plenty of whores. I find it exciting to think about. If I were a man, I'd buy a different one every week. You have them and pay the check, as you would for an excellent meal. You ask yourself each day what does your palate crave, and you simply satisfy yourself and the waiter takes the dirty plate back to the kitchen. There's no need to consider the woman's feelings. You use her and discard her—why not?"

By then, I was as aroused as I had ever been. Was she trying to stir me up, or did she, as it appeared, have no idea how her words affected me? I had made a stern endeavor in the previous chaste weeks not to go to a prostitute, not to relieve myself in any way when an urge presented itself. I had been waiting for her to be ready. Naked, she strolled around the room looking at the quality of my dishes, inspecting the wardrobe that held my suits, getting out my shoes and scraping off a speck of dirt with a long fingernail.

I grabbed her by the wrist, spun her around, me still fully clothed, and forced my mouth onto hers. She yielded at once, and as I pushed her back on the bed, she held both arms above her head, in a gesture of utter surrender.

"Are you going to take me?" I practically tore my shirt and pants getting them off. I feared I might ejaculate before entering her. As I lowered myself onto Valerie, skin touching skin, she brought both palms to my chest and resisted my attempt to pierce her. "Don't you want to tie me up?"

"What?"

"If you don't have thongs, or whatever it is you normally use, just rip my blouse into strips and secure me with those."

"I don't need to do that."

"It's too bad that oar isn't smaller, otherwise it would be perfect for my bottom."

"Is that the sort of thing you like?"

"I have no idea. The two men I fancied had no imagination whatsoever. I've never had a climax except by my own hand. Perhaps that's why I haven't sought out anyone else except you, much less get married. But I know you're depraved, Kilcairn. There is something delightfully wrong about you. Many nasty thoughts lurk in that brain of yours. I want to crawl down into your fevered mind and explore its labyrinth."

I paced the room trying to calm myself. I didn't want to do anything bad to Valerie. No, she wasn't fragile like Cecilia, I had no yen to protect her, as she seemed quite capable of protecting herself. If anything, I was a little afraid of her. Nonetheless, soon I was tearing her blouse into strips, enjoying the ripping sound, as though I were removing the skin from her muscles. Soon I had fastened one of her wrists to the left head-post.

"Kilcairn, stop."

A murderous rush surged in me at those words, as though she had been shrieking to escape, when in point of fact she couldn't have been more composed. "What?"

"I'm beginning to have second thoughts. Once you've tied the knots of my wrists and ankles, I'll be helpless, powerless. And there is a certain disturbed look on your face, as though I had done you wrong—humiliated you in some way."

"I assure you it's nothing of the kind. Remember that it's you who asked me to do this."

"That's right. But answer me this: what's the worst you could do to me?"

"Could? I don't know; rip your head off, flay you to pieces. What do you want me to say?"

"I only want the truth."

"The only truth is I want to ravish you."

"Go ahead and tie me, then and I'll hope that the worst won't occur."

She had sent me into a full-blown fury, my hand shaking so much that I could barely manage the knots. I entered hard, thrust after thrust, as she grunted beneath, like a boxer taking blows. I thought about the knives in the kitchen. I had an almost irrepressible desire to choke her, punch her, to black both her eyes. I pulled back to peer at her face. All I could see on it was a weirdly placid enjoyment. If I had discerned the slightest agitation or fear on her visage, I would have destroyed her. But sooner than I would have liked, I came with a moan that must have sounded horrifying, as though I were the one who'd been gutted.

I rolled off, sweating profusely, onto the mattress. It was the most I'd ever enjoyed sex. I could barely breathe. Valerie didn't seem in any hurry for me to untie her.

"Did you like it, Kilcairn?"

"Yes, a little too much I'm afraid."

"Why afraid? You're only doing what comes naturally to your kind. You needn't apologize to me."

"Did you—have a release, Valerie?"

"No. But maybe next time. The sheer loss of control must feel exciting. You'll be the man to take me there, I'm sure of it."

"I hope so." Inwardly, I sulked and fumed like a child whose homework fell short of the mark.

"Could you bring me a glass of water, dear?"

I got up, fetched the water, and hastened to release her. Valerie drank down the entire glass in gulps, without stopping to breathe.

"You're going to have to go down to the ladies' clothier and pick out a blouse. I can't return home in tatters and shreds."

"I know nothing of women's clothing."

"I'm a medium. Select a color you think will look pretty on me. How romantic it will seem to have you come through the door with a luxurious garment wrapped up in a box with a ribbon."

"Yes, let me get dressed and I'll go."

I had assumed Valerie and I would continue with this style of domination in bed. Rather, we took up again the round of visits, opera, breakfast with Tom and Tina, her nieces and nephews tearing through the house. One of them even referred to me as "uncle." Leeks, potatoes, flour, hydrangeas, a jetty, leather boots repaired and distributed, Valerie's entire clan, including me, posing for a daguerrotype. These were some of the pastimes that occupied the happiest days of my life. All bitterness had deserted me.

One day, at a performance of Salieri's Prima la musica, poi le parole, we ran into Bellington and Priscilla. It was bound to happen sooner or later. Valerie hung on my arm. I simply referred to her as "my companion." She exuded discreet charm, declaring that everyone knew what important philanthropists and patrons of the arts the Bellington family was. Kip stuttered some sort of thanks. Priscilla did not acknowledge Valerie with any word, glance or gesture. However, she never took her eyes off me. In them smoldered a mix of hatred and desire. The brief encounter, however unpleasant, did my heart good. They had the chance to see me attached to a beautiful woman, far more enchanting than Priscilla with her foxlike face and wary walk.

As we descended the steps of Covent to catch a ride, each to his home, in a voice neither brazen nor reticent, Valerie announced to her parents that we might be out late. Her father replied that they were free thinkers, but not that free. "Poppy, don't be awful. Don't you trust me?"

Once in my apartment, Valerie borrowed a silk robe Cecilia had bought for my comfort, not long before our split, but which I'd never gotten around to wearing. Now it was only a bittersweet keepsake. We sat on the mattress, propped up by pillows. She unbuttoned my pants and stroked me slowly, as if she'd found an unlit candle to fondle while she waited to enter the confessional. As I neared a peak of excitement, she would let go, absently, and a couple of minutes later, begin again. This kept me in a state of nerves. At last, she put it back where it belonged, in my trousers, and gave it a few consolatory pats. Then she hiked up the hem of the robe, parted her legs, and led my fingers between them. "I'm going to teach you, Kilcairn, how to truly give a woman pleasure."

I did as she asked. Her breath, quickening, guided my efforts. Her hand lay atop mine until, at last, she let go and I was on my own. "Tell me a story."

"What kind of story?"

"About one of your whores."

"There's nothing to tell, really. Most of it was mechanical."

Part VI

"Some girl, some lady, must have moved you, thrilled you. Tell me about one of your chance encounters on the street. How you picked her up, your stratagems, then what you did to her in bed. Did the night end in laughter or tears?"

"I met a flower girl once. We went to a restaurant and ate hot pie and raw shrimp and oysters on cracked ice."

"Were those oysters as soft as me?"

"Yes."

"Did they taste like me?"

"I can't remember. It was months ago."

"Kilcairn. It's a story."

"Yes, they did taste like you."

"Good. I want them to. Taste succulent, warm and cold on the tongue at the same time. Did you bring her here?"

"I did."

"Did she wear this robe?

She hadn't, but I knew what Valerie wanted me to say. "Yes, that very one."

"Then what?"

"I disrobed her with my own hands. I put the hibiscus tea on, just as I did for you."

"So that's your method? That is how you seduce these women?"

"It's only one woman. Her hair was long and straight. Her body was more compact than yours, the curves more subtle. I drew a bath for her, in the same tub where you lay soaking. These were my preparations for a night of love. Sponging, caring, stroking."

"How lovely. How thoughtful of you."

"When she closed her eyes, as you did, I moved around behind her and knelt, running my fingers along her delicate ears, set close to her head. In my pocket was a silk scarf."

"One you put there on purpose?"

"No, the act was spontaneous."

"All the better. All the more passionate."

"I wrapped it around her neck and pulled as hard as I could. She fought, churning the water, while the life force ebbed out of her."

Valerie trembled against my hand, expelling breath, followed by a short, guttural cry. She took my head in her hands, kissing my lips with small strokes of hers, licking them as if I'd left a trace of honey there. "What a story you tell, my beloved Kilcairn. What an imagination you possess. Someday you must write a book consisting of erotic tales of terror. Everyone in London would buy it, secretly of course. Few will admit to what they really enjoy. What did you do with the corpse? You had to bury it somewhere."

"You finish the tale for me."

"I would have dumped her in the river. Risky, but the Thames is foul, and running water is your friend. With suicides and accidental drowning, your package would just be one more, except of course for the burn around her neck from where you strangled her."

"Could we change the subject? Let's go out. Anywhere but here."

Easter arrived, with its hams and patent leather, starched green gowns, pink and yellow bows, hats more floral than the lilacs in the dooryards. Nostalgia drew me to St. Magnus the Martyr. No doubt Bellington and Priscilla would be in attendance, and possibly Cecilia.

Part VI

I had an overpowering sense that she had returned from France, and of all places she might arrive, and least expect to run into me, was the very altar at which she married me. I had sent to the cleaners my finest worsted suit, let the barber spruce me up and dust me with powder, shined my Oxfords myself, found that my most elegant waistcoat, which had lain enshrouded in a chest of cedar chips, fit well. Sporting a cane I didn't need, I took a carriage to the church. Who knew whether its bright maple, and the crisp jut of my top hat, ringlets falling to either side, the soft weave of my suit, the mineral oil with which I'd rubbed my face to show off its shine of health, would present me as dapper, fresh, worthy of the resurrection of Christ.

Worshipers filed in, silk ties and glossy boots, canary crinoline, or a discreet pearl-gray topcoat, with a matching vest. The collective motion of the ladies' skirts seemed to sweep in the procession, clearing the way for the bishop's cassock. The choir's sustained thrum pierced the incense smoke with a message of eternal life.

I lingered outdoors, off to one side, hoping to spot one or more of the Bellingtons. By the time the Bishop strode in, his white frock embroidered with a rococo cross, the pews were packed, and devotees lined the sides. I scrutinized one face after the next, literally counting my way down each pew. The bishop began to speak of the resurrection. The words he chose were the right ones for this crowd—Espiritus, in nomine Deum, ad aeternam. Scarcely a hiccup had happened in the throat of a newborn that couldn't be soothed with a tonic. Why wasn't Cecilia here? Where had the Bellingtons gone? Did he feel so powerful now that he could flaunt his Savior on the Day of Resurrection?

My eyes had become blurred and I heard myself sobbing as I rushed from the side aisle out of the church, stumbling down steps until I clutched the trunk of a tree. Doves lurched among the stones of the piazza, pecking at seed left by arriving children.

Among a group of painters and musicians, I sat on the floor, back on my legs, like a boy about to shoot a marble. There was little or no age difference between most of them and me. Yet I was the one who felt old, used up, my skeleton twisted inside my slender flesh, as if trying to escape. I perceived myself as existing in some limit at the end of the human species. My introduction as a friend of Lord Houghton, was enough to put them at ease. They had already become elated.

I took a pipe from one and inhaled while he lit the chunk inside the pipe's bowl. The acrid flavor burned into me.

We took turns smoking, me enjoying the simple camaraderie of passing around the pipe. Light invaded the fibers of my muscles, stretching them as though I were a skein of wool. I began to unwind over the floor, down the hallway, in and out of different rooms, a striped housecat chasing me. I vibrated with the acoustic yawn of a cello string. Was I the sort of person whose skin could produce music?

A woman fragrant of sandalwood leaned in to brush my neck with her fingertips. Like a fire that catches at the bottom of a deep pile of twigs and branches, the smolder of my desire couldn't be seen at first. It filtered through as smoke. I was trying to tell her to run away, but on my thick, dry lips, the word leave came to her ears as leek.

"He wants to eat soup," she announced to the small assembly, and they responded with a lazy half-laughter.

"Well, we haven't any here. I already ate a kumquat."

The sandalwood woman led me by the hand into the street. We stopped by a townhouse made of far too many bricks for its occupants, to pick up two friends of hers. Their matching purses seemed an annunciation of destiny and the end of historical time. Stones and leaves rushed past, hedges, thistles and spokes, a handful of oysters held in someone's palm, a cascade from a rain pipe under which we wet our heads, a whinny from the slack lips of a mare, the barn loft in which I first knew the roundness of Peggy, the bawl of sheep beneath us, thunderheads cracking like peanut brittle.

I came to my senses in a vacant field ten miles north of London, surrounded by the sandalwood woman and two others. Their throats had been cut and blood had flowed over the bodies to garish excess, congealing and drying. I too was covered in blood and had shat my pants. I stood up and screamed myself hoarse, not caring whether anyone could hear me, half hoping a passerby would rush into the field.

I located the nearest farmhouse, crept around it, and seeing no one at home, shattered the panes with a shovel I found in their shed. I rummaged through a wardrobe for a suit of clothing and a pair of gloves. I washed myself clean in their bath. Returning to the scene of the massacre, I ripped my bloody garments into pieces, dug three graves, and buried each corpse in one. My garments I burned, before hurling the shovel into a drainage canal.

Late afternoon was turning to evening. I walked through fields before emerging onto a trafficked road. A coach took me to a water taxi, where I crossed the river, found my bed, and slept for twelve hours.

After several weeks of quiet, during which the police—so I heard through the legal grapevine—conducted interviews about the disappearance of Miss Sandalwood and her two companions, a field hand found a shovel with blood on the metal tip and a woman's shoe. The captain who had tried twice to catch me had put himself as head of the case. A cadre of police with hounds spread out over the fields and by the end of the day had found the three graves. The newspapers spoke again of the Gentleman Killer, remarking that he had not been so gentlemanly this time around. There had been beating and mauling. The three, two of them far past being girls, had attended a convent school in Hampstead.

Over a dinner of Cornish hen with Valerie, I related that the police had asked me to come in for questioning. She offered to go along.

"Where were you that night? You were with me. We went boating that late afternoon. The weeping willows were so awestruck by our gilded presence that they forgot to cry. We went home and had several juicy tosses. They'll believe me." It all went down as Valerie had instructed. She gave them just enough delectable bits about our night together to make her, not me, seem the bad person.

None of the cases against the Gentleman Killer got solved. They made multiple arrests with people who more or less matched the profile they were building, men whom they could have easily arrested, to appease public opinion. But they preferred to leave the case open, in the hope that the one perfect suspect, faced with impeccable, irrefutable evidence, would atone for the murders of ten women, connecting them all. To do otherwise would take all the drama out of the situation.

The immediate furor over the case of Miss Sandalwood and the convent schoolgirls settled down, but it did have fallout for me. Gladstone was beginning to reshape Peel's party in his own image, preparing it for an eventual return to power. This time, Gladstone did not call me to his chamber. Instead, he sent a lower level assistant, not much more than a polished clerk, to let me know my services were no longer needed. Perhaps I should have been upset, dejected, outraged, and made a protest, but I wasn't, and I didn't. I had gone too far into Valerie's world, a woman's world, in its essence not compatible with the world of men, business, laws, or government. It is understood among our sex that women are for certain uses and purposes, chief among them procreation, pleasure, child rearing, and keeping the home fires burning. Also, they are to rely on us and not get out of hand, like certain evangelical prophetesses, anarchists, and intractable burlesque dancers who want to rise in the social scale.

The problem with me, as Gladstone surely would have stated it had I asked for his direct opinion, is that I couldn't keep my women in hand. The time he'd run into Valerie and me at a charity event, it was clear he had a low opinion of her overly vivacious nature and her absorption in me. He treated her as if she were a charlatan hypnotist who could only hold inferior minds in thrall. His patronizing remarks and her lightly blistering retorts made me bid goodbye in less than five minutes. The clerk explained that Sir Gladstone had a great appreciation for my talents, and had nursed great hopes for me, but that it appeared I was heading in a different direction from his.

It was the truth. Whatever I could give to Gladstone right then, while energetic, would remain inconstant, as would my attention to details as I managed, as a personal political secretary, his interactions with MPs, the public, and press. That could only happen when I had completely rehabilitated myself as a public man. Not only had I not done that—the very fact that I had been the object of an investigation about murder was evidence in itself that I hadn't been handling things very well. My having been exonerated so far didn't improve matters much. He'd taken a gamble by bringing me into his circle, but if he ended up as Chancellor of the Exchequer in a short time, it would be because he was in fact a prudent man, judicious, his risks calculated down to the minutiae. He picked who he wanted to surround him, mentored and cultivated them, then trusted them to perform without embarrassing him and with very few lapses. If I'd gone to subtly prostate myself before him, promise to mind my manners and do everything he asked, he might have given me one more try.

"Didn't you ever want to revenge yourself on Bellington?" This was the question Valerie asked as I rowed her under a bridge in Hyde Park to the other side, gliding close to the shore so she could inhale the fragrance of cherry blossoms.

"No. He scarcely ever enters my mind."

"How can that be so? He ruined your life."

"Let's say I try not to think about him. If I settled scores, I'd have to include his associates and members of Parliament. And that task would never end."

"He's known as the apotheosis of the bad man. He cheats, bullies, swindles, punishes, and has offended many lives. Even his associates can no longer stand him, and only put up with him because he has so much power. It's a wonder he hasn't been assassinated by now. I'm sure I'm not telling you anything you don't already know."

"I can assure you he's not going to change."

"So, let's kill him."

I picked up my oars and set them in the boat. "You're joking, of course."

"Half-joking." She peeled a tangerine and handed me a section.

"That's not a fit subject for discussion in a public park."

"Then we'll discuss it tonight, in bed. Think about it, Kilcairn. Since the railroad market collapsed, he has accumulated more enemies than ever. Lots of people would like to see him dead, possibly even his own wife."

"Let's leave his wife out of it."

"All I meant to say is that time has passed since he threw you to the dogs. I doubt you'd surface as a suspect at all."

"If we followed the same method as G.K., surely it would be assumed that he'd become active again."

"First of all, Bellington is not a woman. The savagery of the Gentleman Killer has been solely directed toward the female kind."

"So, he's turned over a new leaf. He's a master of surprise."

"You really are deranged."

She laughed and threw tangerine peelings in the water, where they floated. "Am I?"

In bed, straddling me with her powerful legs, squeezing me, hair bouncing wildly around her head as she sweated and crushed my chest with her palms, Valerie brought me to an absolute lather.

"Let's do it, Kilcairn."

"Do what?"

"You know what. The thought of it excites me so much I can barely draw my next breath."

"You're serious?"

"Yes."

"I don't know what to say."

She put her hand over my mouth and stared me down with her cobalt eyes, while the curtains fluttered in the open window, the scent of rain behind them. I could hear drops hitting the leaves, first light and then heavier, and the traffic noise and occasional shouts died off. "Don't say anything," she instructed. "I know you've killed a woman before. Now this is a secret to be shared between us. You make me so happy, Kilcairn. We're perfect for each other."

"I'm afraid that we are."

In the morning, as I basted eggs for us with the kind of thick slices of bacon we ate on the farm, I waited for Valerie to make some reference to the night before. I assumed that the previous night had been a fantasy. She didn't know what it meant to actually murder someone, the soul fatigue of it.

The problem was that she'd set me to thinking about Bellington. He'd taken my money, prestige, and wife, just when I'd made a clean slate. He'd ruined me and I'd done nothing about it. "All right," I said, as if ordering a second drink in a bar. "Let's kill him."

"Darling, you make me so happy."

Valerie and I planned the execution of Kip Bellington. We soon reached the point where we couldn't turn back. We began to rehearse possible scenarios for intercepting Kip and isolating him. A warehouse lay close by, near the wharf. I knew his movements well. We decided that in less than a fortnight, we would wait outside the café where he consumed his "man's breakfast." It was his habit to stroll from there to the wharf and there was a shortcut he favored through a long deserted alley, isolated yet conveniently close to the water. Water or warehouse, either way we had a quick option for stashing the corpse. I had accompanied him on this walk more than once. However, it was an occasion on which he liked to be alone, when possible, to muse on his constant conquest of the visible world, and I believe that this traversal made him feel courageous, daring, gave him swagger, reminding him of his younger days and exploits in certain risky quarters of London. This promenade was all that remained of that concerted youthful vice. And it was the only time I could be sure to catch him alone.

He was punctual about when he left the café, so we wouldn't have to spend time lurking and possibly becoming conspicuous. In the days leading up to Kip's planned death, Valerie ceased talking about it and I did the same. In the final week, we did normal, everyday things, me at my office until three in the afternoon, and in the evenings, we read a book, attended a show, cooked, took a bath, her scrubbing my back with a brush, or just sat on the terrace watching pedestrians in fine dress until the fog came up or they were scattered by raindrops. Never had Valerie been so loving, making me fudge, finishing the sweater she'd been knitting and having me wear it to her father's birthday party, where a cousin played a bagpipe and Tony wept with some unspoken memory.

"Are you ready?"

"I suppose so."

Saint Augustine teaches that the punishment of every disordered mind is its own disorder. That is what I've tried to outrun, with clarity of thought, with precision. I explained calmly to myself that this time I would get caught. Whatever happened, I would take the fall, not Valerie.

I traveled on foot to the Chelsea Old Church, where the Vinegar Bible hangs by a chain, where Sir Thomas More once said his prayers. I considered stepping into a confessional, but I waited first to feel something, anything, that might announce the presence of God. I drifted into the nave, smelled a faint mixture of incense and the ashes of martyrs and heretics. As the bell rang in the tower, I felt exactly nothing. Only sex and carnage, those messy, fluid activities, had filled me with exaltation. I'd always assumed that learning and remembering the words of the great sages would let me float over the trail of corpses, rendering them irrelevant. Bishop Berkeley's philosophical proof that the mind's perception exists prior to all physical reality had appealed to me ever since I first read his words at Oxford. I had ardently desired to live as an idealist, outthinking the muck. But really, I was little more than a creature stuck in the world of animate and inanimate objects, a body with a mind attached like a tumor, controlled by instincts, unable even to point to their origins. I wished, for a fleeting moment that I could enter into the cycle that others call guilt, repentance, and redemption, in the same way I once contemplated slitting my own throat just to see what it felt like. Really, though, they were just words to me, an artificial catechism, rote and mechanical, hands slipping over a rosary as over the vertebra of a victim, the hard nodules confirming that I was, indeed, immersed in a bizarre experiment called living from which there was only one escape.

That night, Valerie gave me a massage over the full extent of my body, with scented oil, probing into every sore spot, as if preparing me for a great athletic event. Never had so much anticipation gone into any single action of my life, not even marriage, entry into Oxford, or my first day in the employ of Bellington. As if sensing the doubts that plagued me, she whispered, "This is the crowning moment, Kilcairn. When the blade comes out of your coat, plunge it in, as you always have, without thinking."

Once in my life my father took me out of Carickmannon, just the two of us travelling together. He filled a wagon with straw, threw packs of provisions on it and bade me ride in the back, in comfort while he drove. His face looked dour, as usual, yet I somehow knew we were headed for pleasure. The sides of the road were strewn with bluebells and daffodils, as well as small purple flowers, the names of which I didn't know. Beyond the flowers lay fields of clover. I lay on my back. In the sky floated puffed-up clouds that I imagined to be larger than the ones that passed over our town. The wagon jolted over rut after rut, the scars left by other travelers, and I felt bad that my father had to receive the brunt of those jolts, while I enjoyed a soft journey. I considered how he slept on the straw tick at home, and that he might be relieved from that austere office, if only for an hour or two. I sat up and shouted to Pa that if he liked, I could drive while he rode as my passenger. He roared with laughter, as if I'd spoken the funniest phrase that one could utter. He assured me that all was fine from his perch, he had a wonderful view of the miles ahead, and that someday I would indeed serve as the driver. I was happy that I'd asked him, just to see his smile and hear his robust laugh, something close to joy.

I'd never supposed that a snow peak existed in Ireland. I had heard one of my father's pals speak of high peaks of ice abroad, in a place called Switzerland, fields of snow into which a man could sink over his head, and deep crevasses into which climbers had fallen, never to be seen again. Our mount did not compare, with only a rime of snow near the top, not entirely covering the rock. Yet I decided ours qualified, that we had our own, not needing to go see theirs, and that in its way the mountain was majestic. I named it Little Matterhorn.

Pa stopped at a farm to ask whether he could leave the wagon and horses overnight. The farmer, although surprised, agreed after a few coins changed hands. Each of us took a cloth pack, mine smaller, and slung the attached rope over a shoulder. I enjoyed the hike through the heather for the first hour, then we began to climb, hidden stones springing up among our feet. I began to complain. He turned around quickly and his arm jerked. Without being able to put it into words, I understood that he was struggling to get out from under an enormous shadow, big as a cloud but not one that would dissolve with rain. There was love in his expression.

"You're a handsome lad," he said. "Try to be glad right now, because this carefree spirit won't always be so. You'll look back on this moment and will even yearn for the burrs that lodge in the wool of your socks right now, as if they were kisses on your ankles from a beautiful girl. But they won't come back."

We continued to hike, for hours it seemed, until we could see a distant lake across the valley, and a herd of sheep spread out on the grassy low slopes beside it. Never could I have believed a sheep could catch the eye, as if I could reach out my hand toward a dandelion that had turned to a white puff, pluck it, breaking the stem, feeling its sticky juice on my palm, blowing the flower's spores to the wind. I then amused myself imaging that each seed would lodge among blades of grass, miles away, and become a new sheep. Of course, I knew how sheep were born, I'd watched their birthing, but I had a different idea, the kind you cling to stubbornly, the more so because you know it's not true.

Long silences accompanied our hike. I didn't mind the stillness, the cooler wind blowing upon us like a caressing hand. Yet the tone of my father's voice, nay, its very timbre, sounded musical, as never before, and I asked him some nonsensical question, just so he would speak again. Deep in thoughts I couldn't have understood even had he explained them, he ignored my question, not unkindly, rather thoughtlessly. I wanted to pick the burrs off my socks, which stung my ankles through the wool, but like the child that I was, I left them there as kisses.

Thirst parched my throat, and as if sensing it, he turned and offered me the canteen. We drank together, taking turns, me making sure not to gulp the water down, as if I were ungrateful for what he had brought for me to drink. We ate fresh cheese, salty and still wet, wrapped in cloth. Even its mild stink was pleasant, as the center of a flower can be bitter, yet you don't want to pull your nose away. You want to become a bee, charged with hopping from flower to flower, mindless, moving only by instinct yet knowing exactly where to go, even if your looping flight looks like confusion.

I loved my father so intensely in that moment that I could have burst into fragments. I wanted him to put his arms around me, to hold me tight, and assure me that there was no specter to fear, that all the strangeness of our household was a quirk, an aberration about to pass.

I tried not to think about my mother and her fits, her black moods, the days she couldn't so much as lift her head from a pillow. Yet other times she appeared frightfully strong, lifting a large canister of milk, pushing back into place a loose barrel stave so that rainwater wouldn't leak out, birthing lambs when needed. How could both these tendencies exist in the same person?

That night, Pa wrapped me in a blanket, tightly like a newborn, made a little fire from what scant timber he had brought and scrounged along the slope. The little flames wouldn't last long, but were enough to warm my feet and face. Pa never got cold, not that I could tell. Shadow cast by the light of the campfire, his knotted hands with their big knuckles rolling a cigarette, he looked powerful, as if he could raise a boulder over his head. Sitting cross-legged, he took out a flute I never was aware he owned or knew how to whistle into, and played some simple Celtic tune, its five or six notes managing to sound as if they could encompass all songs. I was trying to count the stars that peeped out from the drifting clouds, now silver at the edge of the moon, but I was getting sleepy.

I would have dozed off if my father hadn't spoken my name. "Kilcairn."

'Yes, Pa."

"Your mother."

"What about her?"

"She had many hard days as a child. Things happened to her that I can never speak of. They are too dreadful. It doesn't matter whether or not you know the details. She's a good woman at bottom. That's the important thing. Even when you can't stand the sight of her, remember what I have said tonight."

"I will, Pa." I lay quiet for a time, listening to his breath, looking at the cap he wore on his head to keep the sun off. "Father," I said at last, "may I ask you a question? And you won't be upset at me?"

Here came that laugh again, smaller than before, though still genuine. "Ask me anything. Of course, I wouldn't be upset. You're my son."

"Do you and Ma care for each other?"

"In our way. Marriage isn't what you think it is. Yet we endure on the farm, not letting anyone come between us."

I never saw that man of the Little Matterhorn again, not so free. As with the burrs on my socks, I yearned for him many a day, but he vanished from my sight.

I spotted Cecilia, down by the fish market, a strong breeze blowing off the water. It wasn't her neighborhood—in truth, who knew what her neighborhood was now? I assumed that if she had returned, she would be living with her parents, in that perpetual state of dependency she'd grown used to early on and only broken for a short time, while we were married. Then again, maybe they'd set her up in an apartment, to make her feel, falsely, that she enjoyed freedom, as if they'd had a cat they let outdoors to explore the immediate neighborhood, knowing that it would return for feeding and comfort, satisfied at understanding the tacit confines of its geography.

Cecilia didn't look fragile anymore. She'd filled out, carrying easily half a stone in new weight, limbs of at least modest force, her waist not thick, but no longer so tiny. Her hair, that lank waterfall over her shoulders, remained the same. I guess I had expected her to cut it short like those nuns at the convent in Italy where she'd once gone to hide her pregnancy by Wilberforce, before she became morphine addicted.

Now the seller had wrapped the package and Cecilia held it gingerly, looking at me first sidelong, then full on, her eyes serious, as if gauging my depravity—as if knowing the plans I had made with Valerie to kill Kip. I was going to duck down a side street, so that she might believe she had only glimpsed someone who looked like me. But toward me she came, slowly yet with a decided step, like a ghost that had business to attend to one way or another with the living, so it could finally rest. She stopped only inches from me. The fish in her package was fresh, no doubt, yet I could smell its light scent, overshadowing hers.

"Dear Kilcairn. I'm glad to see you."

"Are you?"

"Of course. Yet that sentiment is mixed with bottomless sadness. Do you mind me saying so?"

"No. I feel exactly the same way."

"I'm sorry I ruined your life, Kilcairn. It's the only time I was terribly cruel to someone. What I did was unconscionable. Many times, I thought about rushing to you. I never did, though. And the longer I waited, the more guilty I felt, and that guilt in turn kept me more paralyzed and less able to do it. So stupid. My life has been a tortured waste."

"Don't say that. I don't hold your choice against you. You were always in the grip of someone."

"I blame myself. We always have a choice. You chose better than me, even if your career didn't quite work out. I followed you from afar, and I know from hearsay you were an intimate of Gladstone. I was happy to see you rise again, and I hoped you'd end up in the Cabinet of the government. You know how much I wanted you to stand for the House of Commons, and you would have won if…if Kip…hadn't pushed you aside. You're that smart. You tried to do good things."

"I didn't choose well."

"What do you mean? You didn't ruin your life, as I feared. You didn't go to drink, I'm sure of that. The only thing I can say against you is what happened with my mother—which I'm not even sure ever actually happened. I don't believe her. It was her way of driving you out of my life, and she succeeded. And if it did happen, I blame her. She is the greatest of manipulators, cunning, full of stratagems. And don't imagine she still controls me. I barely speak to her. I have my own house now, and I don't depend on her money."

"Whether or not I ruined my life—that's a matter of opinion. I wish I could sit together for hours and tell you everything, all my misdeeds, my crimes—"

"How you exaggerate, dear husband—sorry, habit. Dear Kilcairn. You are the kindest person I've ever known. You treated me well, made me feel like someone. I'd be an opium addict, probably dead, but for you. I am the one who betrayed you. But let's not argue about it. You look handsome and healthy. I don't want you to feel bad. Whatever you think you've done, you can always change. I did. You must forgive yourself. And if you can't, well I forgive you."

I seized both her hands. "Cecilia, come with me. Let's start over. That's the only salvation I can believe in. I looked for you all over France."

She drew close and stroked my hair. "I wish you'd found me. I would have liked that. But I have a husband and I'm expecting a child. And you probably have a special someone too."

"I didn't know. Anyone is lucky to have you, and you always had pretenders."

"He isn't like you. Not so brilliant, good-looking, ambitious, driven, or attuned to me. And he didn't get me off opium addiction. I don't love him as I did you. But he is terribly kind, he got me away from my parents, as you once did. And though he and I seldom speak to my family, they tolerate him and don't disrupt our lives. Having a child will be the last step to my freedom. If for no other reason, Priscilla being a grandmother will terrify her and keep her away from my offspring and from me. If someone refers to her as Grandmama, I believe she'll have a nervous collapse."

I wanted to wear Cecilia down, to keep talking, to persuade her away from husband, house, security, into the depths of my life, where I would doubtless destroy her. But a point of grammar—her saying did love, instead of love—kept me from insisting. "I'm happy for you. When you went to France, I almost went mad wanting you. But more than that, I worried that you were suffering, and I surely don't want to be the cause of that now. It was only an impulse. May I embrace you?"

"Don't be silly." She threw her arms around me, a long, tight hug, the equivalent of a hundred conversations we would never have, a hundred nights of making love, and days of cooking, strolling the sidewalk, looking on the face of a child made from her and me rather than her and someone else. I could feel her tremble, but I could also feel her strength. She whispered in my ear, "I wish things had been otherwise."

I grasped her hands one last time. "It gives me pleasure that you were able to get pregnant again. Even if it's not mine." I summoned a small laugh, so that my words would come off as a light parting shot.

Kip stepped into the street. A breeze blew up, rustling trees, separating leaves about to fall anyway, and bringing on the earthy scent of rain. With the sky lowering, I suspected that he might skip breakfast. I'd told Valerie to wait inconspicuously on a bench nearby. The weather, crusts of snow still clinging to the sides of the street, kept many people indoors at this early hour, surely an advantage. At the spot of the planned encounter, I could drag his bleeding body in between two buildings, lift myself into the low window of a factory that didn't open for business until later, and leave through a door at the other end. I'd already rehearsed the entry and exit, dragging a bag of flour, and it was simple.

A cat ran alongside me, orange fur lifted, jumped onto a sill and slipped through an open window as I followed Kip at a prudent distance. I'd forgotten how large Bellington was. He did no exercise, yet his broad back bulged beneath the coat. He had a thick neck and I wondered whether in fact a knife would reach his jugular. I'd make a decision on the spot. Already daylight put us at risk. Yet there was no other way to get to him. What I really wanted was to lie abed until a late hour with Valerie watching the inevitable downpour, safe beneath a quilt, feet warm with the coals in a brass pan with a long handle I'd picked up in an antiquities shop. We'd drink tea from a copper pot given to me as a present by one of my Oxford pals, from the blackest packet I had.

Kip arrived at the door of the tavern, which every weekday opened, just for him it seemed, at this curious hour, and whatever stray customer might wander in while he ate. He hesitated, drawing out of his vest a timepiece I knew had belonged to his grandfather, one of the few objects, out of the many he possessed, that made him sentimental. I decided that if he didn't go indoors, if he didn't enter to eat, and continued on to work hungry, I'd let him go. Why this sudden superstition became meaningful, I can't say, yet there it hung, like a bell to be rung on the empty street. Bellington continued, grasping the handle, rattling it, finding out it was locked and turning away. At that moment, the proprietor, in a clean apron, leaned out with a call and waved him in. A smile passed between them, one many years in the offering, the sign of two familiars, neither friends nor enemies, rather the sort of acquaintance that, because it is limited to half an hour a day, can remain warm, unquestioned. Were all our relationships so limited, we wouldn't have time to fall afoul of one another, through betrayals, jealousy, carnal appetites, or the desire for the other to secure us money, renown, political clout.

Valerie had dressed in fur bound to get soaked before we could ever make it back to my lodging, as she hadn't brought any sort of rain cover. I crossed to Valerie, came close, and spoke to tell her I didn't think the day lent itself to our intention.

At that moment, Kip ducked back outside, taking the measure of a light cold rain that had begun to fall. The clouds could not have loomed blacker and thicker. I surmised that he'd only tossed down a hot drink, in his hurry to beat the storm. Indeed, the drops became heavier, almost pelting us, and Bellington began to run, loping, to hasten to work. It was a strange sight, this man who despite his bluster normally possessed a sort of dignity and gravitas, his body now rocking in a purely animal rhythm, as if he'd already been wounded. I turned to wave off the venture, and at that moment, Valerie leaned in, reached her gloved hand beneath my coat to the inside pocket, removed the knife and ran behind him, silent and swift, her shod feet soundless on the stones. I knew she was athletic, but couldn't believe the speed with which she closed the gap between them.

I was stunned and didn't react right away. The two disappeared beyond my sight, from the diagonal where I stood, into the alley. I heard a man's cry, muffled by the rain, and Valerie ran out of the alley, knife no longer in hand. As she drew close, now as ungainly as she had been graceful, she blurted out, "I stabbed him in the back and he fell to the ground. When I saw him getting up, before he could make me out in the downpour, I fled. I dropped the knife in a sewer grate."

"That's not how this is done," I snapped, but there was nothing else to say. Putting my arm around her shoulders, so as to appear as a couple caught out by the weather, I hurried her around a corner, our heads ducked, and we settled into a walk, both of us drenched. We couldn't have hailed a cab had there been one. Instead, we traversed the streets and soon had made it back to my apartment.

Only then did she notice a smear of blood on her glove. Lifting up the hem of her dress, Valerie cleaned it on the inside of the cloth. "I don't want to leave traces."

"That's not necessary, you know. I do have towels. Or you can just throw it away. I don't think you'll be using those gloves again."

Once we'd gone inside, I expected her to have a look of nausea or worry, but instead, she smiled. We hurried to disrobe, throwing our wet clothes on a heap on the floor, the smear of blood on her dress visible, as if she'd begun to menstruate. "I'm going to bind you tightly," she said, "the way you do me."

"Bind me to what? Your love?"

"If that's what you want to call it. I had something more primitive in mind." I took the thongs she needed from a drawer, likewise a gag. She asked for more leather straps with which to bind me, as I was stronger than her, though by how much I couldn't say. "The incomplete kill has left me highly unsatisfied. I'll have to take it out on you."

Valerie set to work in earnest, and before long, I was strung out on the bed. Not even I, with all my practice, could have bound a victim so well. She would progress quickly if she put her mind to it. Into the kitchen she disappeared and returned to the bottom of the bed with another large knife, one just as sharp as the first. She'd watched me use it to filet a steak, then sharpen it again on a stone.

"I'm going to tell you a story, Kilcairn, the best I've told yet, and I want you to listen with care. The evening I dismounted from that cab by the Blackfriars Bridge, I knew who you were. You'd tried to strangle me by the band shell earlier that same evening. It was dark. You came upon me with stealth. The night was beautiful, warm, still, made for walking. I decided to cut through the park. I did hesitate, because being a woman you have to think about those things. I had considered earlier going home with my date, as I really needed a man. It had been a long time since the last.

"Then he opened his mouth and I wondered, why are men so stupid? Is every last one of them this awkward, this conceited? I asked myself, is this the best our nation can do? Have thousands of years conspired to produce this specimen, discreetly picking his nose, after having every opportunity, after all that time at Cambridge, after every advantage since the time he suckled the teat of his Cockney nurse?

"I considered how, if he had his way, this companion would soon be suckling at my breasts, just as he had at his nanny's. Later, if he got lucky with me, he'd practically rush out of the room to tell his mates about his latest conquest, and they'd call him a lady-killer. I excused myself, saying that I wasn't feeling well and would take a cab home.

"I refused his offer of company, and he shrugged and turned back to the opera.

"Then I met a real lady-killer. You attacked me. Providentially,

I was passing a bed of peonies landscaped with a line of stones. I stumbled forward, grasping one to break my fall. You couldn't have known what good reflexes I had, as I whirled around and caught you on the side of the head. You didn't get a good look at me, because you were still feeling the shock of the stone blow. But I got a good look at you, Kilcairn, and I recognized you as the man who had been standing for Parliament, the one who lost the savings of many people in a railroad scam. Then there was Gladstone, a patron you never deserved. I considered calling the police, but I decided I'd rather handle the matter myself.

"Braining you with that rock gave me such a thrill, Kilcairn. I stood outside your law offices, watching you live, satisfaction on your face from some good deed of the day, or perplexity about how you might prevail in your next case. Even though we knew one another, I began to follow you around, just as you followed Bellington today. It was fun, observing you while not being observed by you. I could almost understand why you did what you did. Not the gruesome part, but the single-minded purpose. You could strike, or let the woman go; it was your decision, really. If you let her live and go back to her fiancé, she'd never know how close she'd come to ending her days by the simple fact of taking the wrong street.

"I knew right away at the Blackfriars Bridge that you were the Gentleman Killer. I tried to understand your motives. I thought, he's so handsome, he could have any woman. I was going to possess you. You wouldn't be able to resist my charms, and you'd know what to do with my dark streak, folding it into yours like an egg into batter, the yolk spreading through until it's simply part of the cake. Your taut body would do nicely, as well as the silken brown eyes that contrasted with the blonde ringlets glistening with a light dab of oil.

"The first time we kissed, I cradled your head, and I palpated your skull, touching the scab left by the rock blow. You flinched. I pretended to show concern, and you lied that you'd struck it against the edge of a cabinet, that it was nothing to be concerned about. That feeble explanation contrasted with your physical grace. How enjoyable it was to watch your patience in those first days, as you made no reference to sex, didn't try to seduce me, in a sense, simply stalking me, waiting for the right opening. I said to myself, 'Despite all, the man is a professional. He knows it will happen sooner or later'"

"And the lovemaking—dare I call it that? What a magnificent gift you had to offer. You see, I began to love you, or at least an emotion was attached to my wanting. I'd forget about my desire for revenge for a while. There we were, cat and mouse, in an otherwise ordinary life. I was most surprised that you fell in love with me. I felt strangely jealous of Cecilia. It was the only sorrow you carried on your person, the loss of her. You spoke her name with tenderness.

"It would have been more convenient for me to believe that you were simply a monster. Yet even your slight arrogance and conceit appealed to me. You would have made a great Member of Parliament, except I'm sure they would have resented your intelligence and protected themselves by referring to you behind your back as a peasant.

"So, what to do with you, Kilcairn. Do I desire you? Detest you?"

She'd begun to disrobe, her taut yet generous body revealing itself. She slid her hand up the inside of my leg, to the thigh. "All your escapades that ended in grisly death. With what verve you recounted them, yet without the slightest embroidery, the faintest exaggeration. You didn't throw in an exquisite detail or two in order to complete the picture of prowess. For every man, after all, wishes to be seen by a woman as a hunter. The difference between them and you is that you really are one."

She'd begun to do those things to me that she knew how to achieve with her body, to get the results she wanted with subtle movement and the caress of her cobalt eyes. Her right hand picked up the knife. "But what to do, Kilcairn? Stabbing Bellington to death might have satisfied my blood lust. Stabbing in the back—a beginner's mistake. I panicked and didn't even think to bring your favorite knife back with me. It's not an error you would have made. You called off the attack, right when I needed it most. My craving wasn't satisfied."

I tested the tightness of the restraints, which I could tell would hold fast. "Those thongs are secure. My days of horseback riding and sailing taught me the art of knots. It would be so much easier for me to strike you if you'd only wrestle, or beg half-mutely beneath the gag. But you've too much sangfroid. I ask myself, were I to release you now, whether I'd have a permanent risk of being surprised by you, bludgeoned, strung out on the bed in exactly the way I have you pinned now.

"Grunt through the gag to let me know you want me to release it. When I remove it, struggle and scream. Summon the neighbors with your terror. Then I'll release you from bondage. No? No answer? Do you place so little value on your life? It doesn't matter what you do, really. Your terror would only be an act. You're not capable, Kilcairn, of experiencing the fear that you caused in so many women."

She raised the knife, almost ceremonially, and stabbed me over and over in the chest and the shoulders, without any visible order or method, only sheer fury, her muscled arms sinking the blade deep into my flesh. I can't say whether I shrieked, as before long I passed out.

Part VI

I probably would have been the first to fall under suspicion of having assaulted Kip. Given the posture in which I was discovered, I became the object of newspaper and public gossip about a dirty love nest. If the Bellingtons suspected me of an attack on Kip, they said nothing. There was too much to lose if the nature of my relations with Priscilla ever became known. Besides, I was on the point of death, until little by little I pulled through.

I'll never breathe properly again. The pain of the scars won't go away entirely. Valerie came close to piercing my heart, and could have done so, had she only taken her time. She was traced to the attack on Kip, as well as the one on me, and tried in court. I lied to reporters that I was the one who had tried to stab Kip, which only led them to write further articles about the tortured soul in the love nest who wanted to take the fall for his sweetheart. Bellington tersely denied that it could have been me. He claimed that a woman had definitely been the assailant, and that he left the rest for the law to sort out. He believed in the fundamental soundness of justice in the great and progressive nation that was England. A nation without laws, he decreed, was no nation at all.

I testified on Valerie's behalf, that she was a woman of affection and good character, both of which statements were true. You can be a good person and still do bad things—that's what I want to believe. She sat in her box, dressed in black, as though she were in mourning. She never looked at me.

Valerie refused to testify. The judge sentenced her to ten

years, later reduced to five. The Gentleman Killer won't ever be found. The sensational nature of the Love Nest renewed public interest in fatal crimes. There was pressure on the city government to find him and the authorities made a big show of continuing the hunt. Dozens of citizens offered tips, and some even claimed to be the Gentleman Killer. However, they didn't look the type, as they were fishermen and clerks—not gentlemen.

PART VII

THE GENTLEMAN

I RAN INTO TWO OF THE THREE GRACES ON THE BOULEVARD. Neither was much older than me, but they sat at a café table, beneath a blossoming apple tree, in that short season of flowers when everybody from London to Bath and Stratford on Avon tends a tulip garden, red and yellow. It wasn't so much that the women looked dried up or ugly, just plain. It was hard for me to believe how they had thrilled me. They were eating slices of pecan pie, sipping from porcelain cups, like two respectable ladies whose erotic lives have passed.

They beckoned me to sit down, and their Cockney hash of polite conversation lasted for a few minutes. Then they let me know that the Third Grace had died of dysentery. "So you see, it's not all about a pump handle." This reference suddenly became metaphorical, causing both to titter, and laugh outright at the image they'd evoked.

One couldn't suppress her curiosity. "So, does it still work?"

"Our government? Off and on."

She swirled the tea sediment in her cup, like a diviner.

"You get very well what I mean."

"Yes, if you must know. The stab wounds were in the chest, not the groin."

"So," chimed in the other, "we have no plans for the afternoon. How about a little gymnastics, for old time's sake? If you could handle three then, surely two now wouldn't be too much."

"I'm flattered," I said, "but regretfully I must decline. A client is expecting me."

The ladies nodded sagely to one another.

"So, it doesn't work."

I stood, tipped my hat, thanked them for a pleasant conversation, and left. There was no sense being churlish, after all. I'd been inside them several times, pounding as furiously as if I were a miner searching for a vein of coal. Wistfully, I regretted that I hadn't killed the Third Grace with a quick rabbinical slit to the throat, instead of letting her live only to die from diarrhea and dehydration, begging for her life to end, or else praying, a cross clutched to her chest, that the torment would continue in case she might come out the other side and continue on her melancholy path.

Lord Houghton returned from France, unimpressed with the revolution. "Too many barricades, too few swords. I didn't get a single poem out of the experience."

"How discourteous of them."

"I expected to find you hobbling. But you look wonderful. I apologize for not coming to see you. In spite of my blood lust, I'm not good around wounds and sickness."

"It wouldn't have made any difference."

"I was still a little mad at you for tossing away a chance at riches, fame and power. You're reckless."

"If I were Episcopal, I'd tell you that I paid for my sins. Everything that happened was my own fault."

"May I ask you something? Have you ever killed a man? Whatever the answer, it won't go beyond us. My sense of ethics only extends so far. Besides, I value a confidence more than I do the law."

"A man? No; never."

He smiled as he cut into a rare steak. "For you, it's always about a woman isn't it?"

"Yes."

"We men just aren't as interesting, in spite of holding almost every rein of power. They are the great mystery."

'How are you liking that claret? I find mine a bit stale."

"Tell me, did she do it?"

"Who and what?"

"Don't be coy and make me spell it out, thou child without a slate and primer. Miss Valerie. Did she stab Bellington and then do the same to you, twentyfold?"

"All I'll say is that the appetizer usually comes before the meal."

"You know, now that we are both sitting in the confessional, two atheists of different religions, I will make a confession. I used to think that you were the Gentleman Killer."

"And how did you arrive at that conclusion?"

"In the realm of ideas and careful social observation, you seem the type. Something inscrutable lies in you. A dangerous tendency lurks in the back of your eyes, as though you had an inborn grudge against the world. No amount of verbal magic—and certainly you're one of the best thinkers I've ever met—can soothe the stammer, can wipe out the dirty stain on your shirt, the one where the burgundy spilled. You could have been as great a philosopher as Spinoza or Berkeley, I'm quite sure of that. Their ideas are no more original than what passes through your head as they shave you at the barber. But you have to possess a belief system."

"And I don't?"

"I used to consider you a liberal, in the best sense of the word. Still, stabbing several human beings with a knife, that's the most direct statement one could make, yet it lacks logical rigor. You can't really put it in a treatise. You just let the blood spurt, as do the great generals, in the name of ridiculous supposed ideals that propagate human sacrifice."

"Is that what I am to you?"

"No, old man. I honestly don't know what you are. I'm as much a skeptic as you. I'm just talking to amuse myself until the breakfast gets cold. I blame the French."

"I think it's time for a change of topic."

"I agree. I saw the funniest show at a music hall in Paris. A man recited the Marseillaise while balancing a plate on the tip of his nose. And that was only the beginning."

Part VII

Once I had healed as much as medicine and God could make me, I moved to the west of Ireland, as I had planned to do with Cecilia. The windswept coast suits my soul, even if it makes my bones hurt in the cold season. I walk among the rocks at low tide looking for anemones.

I no longer have any instinct to stalk and murder. It vanished. The will for it just went out of me. My neighbors describe me as shy and polite. A couple of lasses, of the type who want to tend and nurture a man, to make him better, have tried to strike up a romance with me. From my many small attentive gestures and the wounded expression on my face, they tell me that I'm sweet, good-looking, gentle, kind, thoughtful, and reflective. I'd like to believe them.

One of the lasses invited me to her cottage, its white paint bright despite continuous beating from the sea. We drank tea, we ate a scone, we shared a smoke, and before I knew it, she lay recumbent in a claw-foot tub while I shampooed her hair. My fingers, still nimble after all, roamed over her face, her ears, her neck, caressing as she talked about the flowers she'd purchased at the market. I poured water over her head, watching the soap dissolve into suds as it ran back down into the bath. After a time, she complained that the water was getting cold. The lass stepped from the tub, and I enveloped her in a big, rough towel. We slipped under the flaxen covers of her humble bed and did together the things that each of us was born to do.

Discuss this Book

1. What in Kilcairn's upbringing allows him to become articulate, eloquent businessman and politician? Does this same upbringing provide clues to his penchant for murder? How do these two very different people co-exist in Kilcairn?

2. How might the story unfold differently had Priscilla not seduced Kilcairn? What role does Cecilia's corrupt father play in Kilcairn's actions and the failure of his marriage to Cecilia?

3. How does Kilcairn justify his serial murders? Or does he?

4. What do Kilcairn's confessions tell us about the era? What do they tell us about the man?

Additional discussion starters for this book and other City of Light titles are available to download at

CityofLightPublishing.com/librarians-and-educators/resources/discussion-guides/fiction/